The
FANTASTIC AFFAIR *of* DESPAIR

Doorva Devarshi is a writer and editor. Formerly a dentist, in 2020, she decided to switch her scalpel for a pen and hasn't looked back since. She lives in Jaipur with her parents and their family's greatest feline obsession, Chimken.

The FANTASTIC AFFAIR *of* DESPAIR

DOORVA DEVARSHI

PICADOR INDIA

First published in 2025 by Picador India
an imprint of Pan Macmillan Publishing India Private Limited
707 Kailash Building
26 K. G. Marg, New Delhi 110001
www.panmacmillan.co.in

Pan Macmillan, The Smithson, 6 Briset Street, Farringdon, London EC1M 5NR
Associated companies throughout the world
www.panmacmillan.com

ISBN 978-93-6113-098-4

1 3 5 7 9 8 6 4 2

FSC
www.fsc.org
MIX
Paper | Supporting responsible forestry
FSC™ C016779

Typeset in Dante MT Std by R. Ajith Kumar, New Delhi
Printed and bound in India by Replika Press Pvt. Ltd.

To the majestic creature in my life, my cat, Chimken

PART 1

THE NARRATOR

ONE

The mackintosh coat is rubbery and uncomfortable. There is not enough shelter in the tent, and its flaps slap and wave in the storm, drenching the two huddled figures inside. Her clothes were soaked a long time back, and the coat is a mercy from Edwin, her companion for this part of her story. Hunkered down and waiting as they are, she eagerly expects the deluge to unleash one within her. She wishes to lament the days past – her time in the city of frescoes with trailing and kind Mahendra; playing cowrie with bloated Leela, her laugh as lilting and consoling as the burbling of the emerald waters of the nearby river that thundered down from ancient glaciers; cooing to newborn Kamal whose eyes widened at every swallow that fluttered close over their heads and every cat that dashed between the huts of the *dharamsala*.

She waits but struggles to remember the times that have gone past. They have left a gnawing feeling in the pit of her stomach and another of a desperate longing in her heart for times that could have been. Now she can only focus on the irksome sensation of the coat on her bare skin, hear only the ear-splitting rainstorm outside, and feel only the splashes that rain on her face through the inefficient cover of the tent. So far in the valley – and consequently so close to the beast – she cannot even locate the rudimentary cognizance that has plagued her in the last few days. The beast knows that she is close, and there is no need to call her any longer. It too waits in its cover of granite further up in the mountains. It waits for the day to clear and for the bed of orchid and primrose to shake off the last of its dew in the sultry sun. It waits for her.

When she forces herself to reminisce, she gets ahead of herself. Days in the valley mingle with the days at the magazine; those at the magazine with the stories of bandits and marauders from her mother's childhood. She is an English tobacconist, wheezing in the early hours of the day. An old, lanky man in nothing but a threadbare dhoti and white undershirt hurries to the bedroom and holds out a bowl of bronze into which she expectorates globs of phlegm before expunging herself of a slimy blood clot. She is a dancing girl in the court of a lowly king of a small kingdom, somewhere in the burning climes of the desert – he showers her with jewels and muslin. She walks purposely along the paved kerbs of New York City, avoiding looking into the eyes of squatters and the homeless, while admiring the neck-breaking giants in the sky and the promise of riches and fame. For a moment, she is even Aarav, forcing down an unwilling body into the depths of a fluffed-up, expensive pillow.

The tobacconist and the dancing girl are not her memories, nor the memories of those whom she will remember now. Beyond the walls of her small village and the three cities she inadvertently found herself in, she has not moved around enough in the world to know much beyond herself. She doesn't know much of herself either, but she hasn't had the need to until now. This part of her story is not her story either, but she will pass without knowing it.

But a story needs a reader, a viewer, a listener. There are eleven other men in her vicinity, separated from her only by the sheets of rain that sting like an angry swarm of bees if she steps out. In this closed space, there is Edwin, whose name slips on her tongue and comes out in a garble. He butchers her name too, until she begins to think that he is addressing someone else. The tall, imposing man does not seem like the kind to lend an ear to someone grappling with a burgeoning need to purge herself of all that has transpired. He frequently parts the flaps of the tent to look out at the storm, as if his loyal vigilance would shame nature into giving way to the white man who has come to conquer it. He grumbles with every passing moment and every spray that drenches the front of his shirt, which has now changed colour to the dark brown of the earth. Even if he were a listener, the two do not understand each other's languages. He knows a few words, which he sometimes throws in the general direction of the sherpas accompanying him, though they do not know these words either; they have learned to recognize the needs of the climbers from the ferocity and velocity of their words.

In these forlorn circumstances, she manages to unleash a flood of memories and events that she must remind herself of to cover that last distance that lies between her and the beast. She yearns to relive that life that squeezed the will and bliss out of her and left behind only a husk that demolished the will and bliss of others. If in these moments, pouring heavens and chafing fabrics are her last sensations, would this journey have been worth the despair? Her stomach coils from an emptiness it doesn't wish to accustom itself to, and her muscles waste – for once, not from the lack of use, but from unexpected, sustained abuse. Her journey is coming to an end.

✿

This story can have many beginnings – a thread unspooling and its bearer drawing further and further until she is out of sight and relegated to lores of mothers and grandmothers and their great-grandmothers. We can start with another 'she' who bore children before her small body had shed the last of its own childhood, or with a 'she' who spent her lonesome days in splendour, surrounded by the opulence of gilded boxes and silvered windows reflecting a queen in name but a pauper in affection. We can even start with a 'he', burdened with early resentment for responsibilities, stuffed as a toddler with preconceptions about those he loves and who nurture him.

This beginning of a 'she' is the beginning of the moment with the mountain climbers in the remote forests and verdant valleys of the Himalayas. She is a young woman in her blossoming years who lies breathless on her cot in her family's hut. The yearnings of a maiden have been discarded for the passionate embraces of lovers. It has only been six months since he arrived in their village – a slightly older boy with rippling muscles and bronze skin, which shimmers and blinds; drops of sweat like water from the trickling streams. He is a timber feller, and she often watches him from the cover of ancient deodars. He has seen her, but he is shy and reserved, averse to the possibility of futile pursuits. He works further and further towards the edge of the forest until he senses her presence between the trunks – which he will eventually axe – and no other person. He grips his axe harder, lets his muscles bulge and tense; he pictures her gasping at this shameless display, and much like her, he too lies uncomfortable, oppressed by the very need that he subdues.

But such beginnings rarely have early ends. She is emboldened by the performance she rightfully believes he affects just for her. She hops from bole to bole while he chops faster and faster, and one day, they meet in the clearing. The forest rests under a shroud of new snow and the English have retired to the warmer plains when the young lovers are married in a brief ceremony. The young man, unable to draw his face into a sombre acceptance of his matrimonial bind, beams at the good luck that has marked a new beginning in his birth charts. The young girl, now armed with the knowledge of domestic obedience, hoists her trousseau onto her shoulders and runs into the arms of her husband. The two begin their journey back to his village as soon as the rituals are over. Under a snug and luminous canopy of chir, they begin their new lives in a small house where his senile and widowed mother learns to ignore the passionate sentiments of the zealous couple.

She is a daughter of nature, as at ease kindling a fire from carefully preserved firewood at the height of moist winters as she is at picking out the right roots and flowers for medicine when the ground clears and bursts with infinite blooms. Her mother has taught her the ways of the mountains; she has committed to mind the sharp, winding leaves of the yew and the deep pains that they relieve for her frail mother-in-law; she dries and prepares the stalk of the sweet flag, fished out from the humid cover of the forest, for her neighbour's man, who violently coughs through the night. She nibbles at the smooth surfaces of berries dropped from the thick beaks of barbets and follows the merry trails of honey birds.

Her days in the lap of the forest she loves, which seems to caress her with contentment, at first make the villagers marvel. They admire and supplicate. However, when a few years pass and nature does not reward her with its abundance, eyes widen with questions and whispers begin to follow her. On cold nights, her husband embraces her lovingly, sometimes wiping her tears with gentle kisses. After seven years, they are still young, but the man gives up hope – not with a broken heart or after locking away his dreams, but rather with love for the woman whose care and affection never wane.

She is, however, not one to be easily swayed by the bilious murmurs of others. Her mother, though now gone some years, had taught her to run and grab what she desired. 'Nature is abundant and gives enough to everyone,' her mother would say. She has grasped in her willowy fist the eternal love of a good man. She has built herself a house that stands the furies of nature. She cannot accept that she is barren. From her forays into the forest and the hoard of knowledge that her mother has passed on about its wonders, she believes there is a cure for their predicament.

Beyond their home of towering chir, there is a forest of bhanj, and somewhere in the nearby sprawling village, she has heard of a woman who prepares concoctions to relieve the ills of the womb. Her journey is to be no more than five days long – passing by the village where she had once resided, now denuded of its cover; the outpost of the timber company abandoned; a thundering river that froths at the edges and only passable by a new metal bridge; thicker woods that were known to home mauling beasts and angry bears. She says goodbye to her husband, letting her hand slip from his grasp, to instead hold that of nature, which she believes will convey her safely to the woman near the bhanj forest.

It is fifty-four days before she returns home. Her grieving husband has travelled to the medicine woman five times in these months, axed down the thickest parts of the forest and sent many men into others. His mother, who loved her like her own daughter and wouldn't eat unless served by her, has died of a broken heart. But she arrives, untouched and unscathed, from the spot she left. Her red sari reflects the early morning light like a sheet of gems. Her feet, though bare, are soft and uncalloused. She only smiles at the villagers who gawk at her, and giggles at the women and children who scream and run away from the ghost risen from the dead. She does not wait to decipher the shock on her husband's face before gingerly grabbing his unmoving hand and leading him into their home.

This beginning of 'he' is the beginning of *The Narrator*, the haunted grounds where the first part of her story unfolds. He is Bablu Nath Mehta, an unfortunate name if there ever was one. Born into a rich family of diamond traders, his ancestors had shaken hands with the white overlords early on. Bablu Nath, as a young child, spends his days running around the grounds of his family estate, brandishing a stick that fills the servants with the fear of the devil. They often watch him whittle away at the ends of small branches snapped off the wasting and diseased trunks of laburnum that line the cobbled driveway. Dulari, the hunchbacked leader of the maids, yanks his arm when she catches him immobilizing a small puppy with a knobby knee with his hand around its muzzle. He is about to impale the rear end of the puppy with his rotting bayonet when Dulari pulls him off the dog. It belatedly snaps at him before dashing beyond a wall of oleander on uncertain feet, propelled by its whimpers and cries.

Dulari is given leave the next hour but at least Bablu Nath does not whittle again and does not dare approach dogs for life. Bablu Nath is not a cruel child – he likes to bite the end of his mother's sari by way of apology because he is uneasy at her angry slight of him; he walks behind his father on the rare days he is at home, repeating the difficult Latin names of the flora of their estate because he likes the rumble of laughter that shakes the older man's chest. But he has seen Dulari's husband perform a similar manoeuvre on the other maids in the Mehta's employ and his pliable mind concedes to the curiosity of performing such an action himself. He expects the puppy not to wail or scream – like Bijauri and Anju – and its howls from beyond the bushes fill him with a lifelong dread. In those days, however, Bablu Nath has much to see and many years of subconscious absorption ahead of him, so such germinal moments soon recede into the depths of his mind.

Bablu Nath does, however, grow up to be a cruel man. The days of laughter on the laps of his grandparents, his dimpled cheeks pinched affectionately, become memories of someone else until they are forgotten – except in the stories of his parents. When they hear of their adolescent son forcing himself onto his cousins and sisters, they wonder what happened to their boy. Bablu Nath is suffering at the hands of others and causing suffering to more. His boisterous friends are amused at the naivete of his name; the fat arms and stomach folds of infants that it brings to mind. They make filthy, childish sounds at him, worsened by any protest. Bablu Nath clenches his fists as he walks back home and only when he has snapped the latch closed on his room does he let the angry sobs flow unbridled. These are days of honours and respectful designations being bestowed on figures who fight for a collective 'us' – another story, perhaps, for another narrator – and inspired by them, Bablu Nath too tries them on for size. There's Chacha, Dada, Guruji. He keeps a list of these names he hears from the mouths of his elders, shovelling them into a remote corner of his desires.

In the meanwhile, his voice and those of his friends break – they become rough, coarse like gravel under the soft soles of feet. There is now 'she' – easier to molest. They have some experience of it. They have watched their fathers and uncles and older brothers – and in Bablu Nath's case, Dulari's husband. The girls knit their brows and adjust their clothes when the boys whistle at them, grab each other's hands and scurry away when someone runs to grab the end of their braids or frail wrists. They dare not protest or convey their discomforts to their families, lest their future days become more hazardous – or worse, their schooldays be brought to a grinding halt. Bablu Nath is relieved – no more the easy target – and after many years of carefully preparing for harder years, he forgets the list of names until they become memories of a different version of himself.

Bablu Nath at this moment is still a young adolescent. He craves that which haunts most children of disengaged parents: love, attention, dedication. His sisters and cousins cry to his parents about straying hands and disrobed crotches, flashes of erect penises belonging to Bablu Nath and his friends appearing in their doorways; for a young 'she' of seven, it is fingers prying into her flesh while Bablu Nath convinces her of the ordinary nature of it. With each passing month, Bablu Nath's behaviour – catalysed by his escalating hormones and the inquisitiveness of his friends who do not have the luxury of easy access to young girls in their own homes – worsens. Incidents rise and aggravate. With every disdainful glance from his mother and flash of subdued anger in his father's eyes, Bablu Nath pushes the limits of their abandonment – until 'she' of seven, bleeding and broken, is rushed to the family doctor.

And so it is that the fate of Bablu Nath is sealed with the fates of several others at *The Narrator*, including the 'she' who now works to create a semblance of a story to recite to herself.

TWO

Many decades later, she steps into a burning room with the month's dummy copy in her hands. In these years, a new epoch has rung in the adolescence of the country. She is born in the days of chuffing chimneys in the distance that fill their mornings with the smell of burning jaggery. Her school teaches the history of only twenty years past – in English. She learns that she is proficient in the language, the grammar of it snuggling into her memory like cats sleeping comfortably in dark corners. Her university teaches her the works of Shakespeare and Hardy, Dickens and Lawrence – occasionally Raja Rao and Bankim – in the colonial tongue.

Along with the dummy edition, she has several copies of articles sent in by the editorial staff. Mahesh, the newest journalist at *The Narrator*, has vilified the work of a Colombian writer. He is angry at the writer's disconnected trains of thought; his traditional sensibilities bristle at the lives of young women stripped down to explicit detail; his disbelieving tirade against the bizarre plot trajectories is barely understandable. She could worry over the dangling modifiers and syntax, but he can hardly tell the difference between 'they' and 'them'. She feels she has been marking and correcting the same mistakes every month. She fears that her mind is failing her.

It has been seven months since Mahesh joined the editorial team, and two since she approached Kumar, their editor-in-chief, about the recurring mistakes. If she didn't know better, she would think that Mahesh's mistakes are deliberate – meant to incense and instigate. But he is just a fledgling, a small fish in an ocean of other improperly educated adults who believe in the inherent power bestowed upon them by what dangles between their legs.

The marketing and advertisement department is not in the same building as the headquarters of *The Narrator*. Chief – the founder of *The Narrator* – wished for the latter to be cocooned in literary purity. Clacking printers and the metallic tang of ink were never to taint the house of intellect. The advertising team is shunned into a small office at the end of the street, along with the typesetters who work on daily papers and the slow trade of books commissioned by the newly emerging publishers in the city. She is now accustomed to making the journey. There is a woman there, Richa, small and plump like her mother. Her nose is permanently marked with a triad of lines from carrying the weight of her large, distorting glasses. Richa isn't her friend, but she has become used to sitting beside her typesetter's table, listening to the rhythmic rattle of her fingers on the keyboard and resting to the pulsing music of it. Richa and she rarely engage in conversation. The former is shy, a woman of few words – if any at all – and has the concentration of a saint. If her nose is buried in the keyboard, there is not much that can distract her from the priorities of the moment. And that's true for most of the hours she spends in the typesetter's office.

She has begun to enjoy the easy silence between them. Once she collects the dummy copies from the marketing team, she climbs the stairs to the second floor. A clerk hands her a steaming cup of tea, after which she wordlessly leaves the office and returns to the odorous halls of *The Narrator*.

But today, Richa isn't there. Her stool is neatly tucked under her worktable. Her large bag, always filled with a fine selection of Mills & Boon romances, is not beside the desk either. Richa has not shown up to work at all. She is slightly bothered by the missed opportunity to relax with someone who seems as misanthropic as herself. She has started to believe that Richa's isolation stems from a past as agonizing as hers. They have not talked about their lives and the rare times when they exchange a few words, it is mostly regarding some enticing news that has shaken the city. She simply turns around and leaves. At that moment, she does not sense the slight shifting of the motes of her universe. The sunlight flickers at the edge of her hair as she steps into the street. The rickshaw puller swerves just in time to let a cat pass, and a woman with a basketful of nearly spoiled vegetables jumps over a puddle of filthy drain water.

✿

This beginning is perhaps the most important beginning in this story. It is the beginning of *her* – the careful curator, the trembling narrator, the woman now leaving the typesetter's. She is still a small child when she is prematurely pushed into the horrors of adulthood. But there are a few years when she is as bright as sunshine; as boisterous and spirited as the bulbuls that joyously chirp from deep within their grove of jujubes.

Her parents and grandparents are careful not to say too many favourable words in front of their other children, but it isn't too difficult to notice the softening of their eyes at her games and the subtle gifts showered on her since her early days. She is their most beloved. As the youngest child, she finds contentment in her own company. Her imagination is ripe and wide, and she carries in her mind a beautiful roster of games to keep herself occupied. She runs through their small garden without shoes, unbothered by the thorns that occasionally pierce her tender soles and unconcerned by the scorpions that frequently sprint out from behind sacks of grain and abandoned bricks.

Nature doesn't love her as it does the woman of the valley, but she – the child – has found an easy existence alongside it. As long as she looks from a distance, the scorpions don't sting, and the thorns move away from where her feet might land. Sometimes she wishes to get closer, but these are not the gentle, undulating valleys. She is born in the harsh flatlands and wide swathes of dried plains that can be spied from miles and miles away – the only hindrance to surveying any further being the curvature of the planet. The plants and trees are sparse. There are not enough months in the right seasons for them to flower and fruit, and they spend most days in a state of wretched desiccation. Their leaves fall and merge with the earth, and they remain in such nakedness, waiting for the first burst of rain that lasts no more than a few weeks.

In such dejected conditions, most of her love for the marvels and wonders of nature grows from books that her father brings from places far away. It is a quarterly event that fills the three brothers and two sisters with unrestrained excitement. The children are readers; she, a collector of knowledge and languages. There is much she wishes to learn and she keeps a long list of curiosities that must be answered within the next quarter. The father is a busy man during the few nights before he is to begin his journey. She is unrelenting in her demands. 'I saw a squirrel with only three stripes on her back. Why only three? Why does the one in our garden have five?' 'How does the cactus know it is in the desert?' 'Why are scripts different?' 'Why do some words sound similar even when they are not related?' Her father and mother tire easily of her insatiable hunger, but could there be a prouder moment for families treading the line between traditional beliefs and Western ambitions?

It isn't uncommon for the spark of childlike wonder to be snuffed out in adults. The harshness of the world beyond the safety of home and the fading words of loving guardians give way to the insolent dictates of misguided authority. The heart hardens, and the small delights of childhood are abandoned for survival, which must now rest on the youthful shoulders of the new generation. It is rather unfortunate that it is just as common for that light to go out even earlier – at fifteen, at ten, at seven, or even at three.

She is nine years old when her uncle, newly a resident of the house in search of jobs at the nearby mills, comes to her room. He has a big smile and large hands. He is dark like coal, with small flecks of brown peppered across his face. He keeps a moustache that her mother often asks him to shave. 'It makes you look like a filmy villain,' she laughs. He sits on her bed and asks about the book on whales she is reading. There are no narwhals where she lives – none outside the borders of her country, or even 'continent', as she has recently learned. But she has safely tucked this odd creature into her mental drawer of curiosities that must, one day, be explored further.

She is only too happy to explain to her uncle the nature of this peculiar animal. 'It has a horn. But it's a fish. But not really a fish. Rather, a mammal of the ocean. There are a few of them,' she says. Her legs swing from her bed, fuelled by the happiness of newfound knowledge. Her uncle wants to know more. He slides a hand under the heavy book. It is warm against her small thighs, even through the fabric of her frock, and warmer still when he lifts the cloth. It is however heavy when it slides further towards her abdomen. She tries to curl into herself, instinctively aware of an unfamiliar and atypical intrusion. But it doesn't go any further that day – nor for a few weeks after. And in that time, her heart stops racing in alarm, and she even convinces herself that, perhaps, it is not unusual.

✿

Five years at *The Narrator* trundle past slowly. For the first two years, when she still shares a desk with Chief's secretary, Kavita, she harbours, if secretly, some hope. She lets the dreams of her childhood and the ambitions of her young adult years fuel the pace of her days. Chief is an enthusiastic boss, more interested in showing up international magazines of a similar tone as *The Narrator* than creating something reasonable for the home ground. Kavita spends most of the morning hours uncovering the plethora of magazines and newspapers that come from thousands of kilometres away. The editions are weeks old, and consequently, the one-up is never on time. Even if it were, Chief's battle was one-sided; the cultured periodicals of the world completely oblivious to the war he was waging.

'Look at this one on Tagore's short stories,' he said, tossing a glossy magazine, one day. The gathered editorial department remained quiet, confused and apprehensive.

'We can write better than this, can't we?' he said, peering over his pencil-thin glasses, anxiously folding and unfolding the magazine in his hands.

When Chief was in the throes of such passions, it was better to recede into oneself. She had learned this the very first time she had sat with him at his Italian teakwood desk. Chief was loquacious, fond of his own voice and further exalted by the inflections and dictions of it. He liked big words and drawn-out soliloquies – but only from himself. Discussions incensed him. Opinions were not for others. An empty ideas board often pushed him into frustrated mumbling about the 'useless brains' he had hired, but any addition to it was promptly removed with derisive words.

She waited for his command – the next direction that would change the course of their week. The staff would burn candles well into the night, reworking the edition that was slated to print in less than ten days. It showed in the way Jagannath swayed on his feet, even if it could be blamed on the local alcohol he had by bottlefuls from morning to night. It was in Kumar's fingers when he ran them across his already balding pate, and in the quiet clicks of Kavita's tongue. She would be the one running between desks and offices – the only line of communication between the team here and the advertising one at the other end of the street.

'We know our Tagore better,' he said. 'We will do a literary homage to all his works – novels, stories, essays, poems, whatever there is.' He rose from his chair and wobbled towards the idea board. With one sweep of his hand, he erased the vision that was ready to meet its printer, chalk dust flying and settling on his feet, shoulders and nose.

'We will show them we can do a better job.'

Chief's impulsivity inspired frequent exasperated whispers across desks and long smoke breaks. But Chief's vision – however aping and foreign it might have been – was so vast and unachievable that every hand was needed on deck. Richa was once asked to contribute to an edition on the twentieth anniversary of Independence. In the high-ceilinged and relatively cooler halls of *The Narrator*, she looked perplexed at Chief's demand. Her family had once resided in Mussoorie and he expected a long essay on the developments that had changed the face of the hill station in the new era. Richa had never been to her mother's hometown, but under Chief's glare, the typesetter had researched and written a copy that had to go through many hands and eyes before it was ready to be sent back to her.

For a while, she believed that her career would one day propel her towards better things. She borrowed, with Chief's permission, one of the unused and abandoned Smith-Corona DeVille typewriters from the office. At home, she ran her fingers over the sleek keys and sleeker still, the bars. She sniffed at the pads of her fingers, which came away with oily black ink. Back then, she believed she had much to say, and from the monthly works she was contributing to the magazine, her future – for once – was not as bleak as she had envisioned it to be.

Now when she makes her way back to the headquarters of *The Narrator*, she thinks she should have had the foresight. Since the days of her uncle's visits to her room, some misfortune seemed to have befallen her. Good tidings never last too long, but bad luck seemed to be the ammunition to her existence.

✿

One delivers and one receives. The luck that shuns her once rained blessings on another. Bablu Nath – our young miscreant from before – has jumped over a hurdle that has plagued him for many years. When he matriculates, there is much celebration. The younger boys in his school are ecstatic that the rich heir will no longer smack their knuckles with a cane or shove their faces into dirty basins until their noses fill with sullage. They are happier still that his companions – brutes of a worse kind – are leaving, their actions best suffered through and not spoken of.

The girls from the school across the road are even merrier. There are other delinquents spreading their wings among the lower-class men, but for now they don't have to look over their shoulders when they leave the grounds or wear scarves that leave not even the skin of their noses on display. They are yet to learn that the scars left behind by Bablu Nath and his friends fester in the younger boys, and their mischief will cut deeper than their now-graduated nightmares.

In the years since Bablu Nath's upper lip first sprouted wispy hairs and his face erupted with pimples, his parents – once distant and proud – become eager to send him away, and with him, the knowledge of his actions. They have ferreted away their young daughters and nieces into boarding schools and the guardianship of relatives in far reaches of the world. The seven-year-old is sent to an institution for many months before she is safely tucked into her seat on her first flight to the crowded world of Bombay. She grows up quiet and melancholic, though not privy to what causes her such sadness.

Bablu Nath, on the other hand, walks a plank and jumps onto a ship bound for New York. The family company bristles at news of the East Africa Campaign: brutal wartimes and troops racing over potential mines with their tanks and guns. Bablu Nath would receive a degree at the end of the war, but his father believes it is better to be prepared. They need good lawyers – learned in the laws of international lands, with accents so refined and skins so fair that the company's new forays into a new continent are not declined.

The young man has grown up in an ancestral home nestled in the bustling city of Ahmedabad. Their house, though large and sprawling, and never in want of anything, has an outhouse for daily ablutions. The women cover their heads at the sound of footsteps they learn to recognize as belonging to patriarchy. Girls past twenty, if unmarried, are considered anomalies – unwanted monsters to be handed over to men twice, thrice their age by way of consolation.

So it is that the more modern proclivities have Bablu Nath's eyes widening in wonder. The mansions and townhouses of the city are closed to him, and for the first time, he finds himself lodged in quarters smaller than those of his servants back home. Though money flows in from home – monthly money orders, sometimes following each other within a week – it does not buy him access into places he truly desires. A sign on an oak door leaves him unattended, cold from both the chill and the disrespect. 'No coloured allowed'. He closes his eyes and imagines the gathering – a hallway marked with a hat hanger, leaning under the light weight; the soft chime of silver cutlery, reminiscent of home; the staccato laugh of the host; middle-aged Fitzgerald holding court on the other side.

But that is all overlooked for the flood of freedom that is Western society. Freedom, which means he wanders the streets in the darkest hours of the night with no fear of his father's wrath at his absence. Freedom shaped like a bottle in a brown paper bag. Freedom to exist outside the incestuous norms of a family business. From the ancient halls of his classes, he dashes into the streets and towards the harbour. Men with important-looking suitcases and women in flowing skirts that leave the milky skin of their calves demanding the gazes of passersby – become the small joys of his everyday people-watching routines. He memorises the flick of their wrists when hailing a boy for a boot polish, and the gratuitous cloying smile as sweet as his coffee from cafés.

For years, Bablu Nath gives himself over to learning the ways of this world – their clothes, their mannerisms, their claims of abundance and justice. It does not come easy or without peril. The park where he unwinds leaves him exposed to discriminatory eyes. A group of picnicking women set a policeman on him. When he awakens, the cuffs are already on him. In the cell, he curses the Black man. 'Criminals, they all are,' he remembers the words of his friend. Pleas and bribes and the summons of a white friend later, Bablu Nath returns to his room, seething but exhausted.

He is a man possessed, going from sale to sale in search of stories – Steinbeck, Hawthorne, Fitzgerald. He piles editions upon editions on the stairs leading to his apartment. He avoids Baldwin and Hurston. He travels to the farthest reaches of the state in search of local newspapers, committing to memory their finest details – their fonts, the spaces between the letters, the mistakes of the typesetters, the wavy flow of their sentences, and the missing U's and A's, in rebellion against their embarrassingly Third-World imperial origins.

In the dead of night, when he retires to bed after a last glimpse at the morning's newspaper, his heart races and his eyes water with a carnal appreciation for the better men on this side of the world. He puts himself to tired and satisfied sleep, picturing the determined hand that wrote so freely – so blasé, so unconcerned with the retaliation that might befall at any moment. The conviction and intellect it must take!

THREE

Outside the cacophonous headquarters of *The Narrator*, she barely steps out of her one-room lodgings in Mrs Pradhan's house. Not much can be said of her belongings – once suggestive of youthful expression of individuality, now discarded and abandoned on the streets, and sold to bargaining buyers for meagre sums. Over the years, she removes more than she acquires, and soon the room is devoid of any personal touch, as if no one with thoughts and desires and passions had ever lived in it. There is a rickety iron charpoy that replaces the cot provided by Mrs Pradhan when she feels that she has no more blood to give and no more patches of skin that do not burn with a vengeance. When she turns over the dusty mattress one day, the crawling and disturbed display flares her body into goosebumps.

In an ala, she keeps several tin jars, which now sparkle from the passage of time, washed away of any remnants of what they might have once held. She has not stepped towards those few possessions in a long time – there are no buyers for them, and she does not appreciate the way the *kabadiwala* looks at her the few times she relents and passes on more of her belongings to him. There is one plastic container, brown and with a peeling label – unreadable after the months it has basked in the sun that falls directly on it – that she once considered a small joy in her otherwise lugubrious existence. In the rings of its lid and the farthest reaches of its bottom, there is still some fibrous chicory. It clings to the surface like barnacles.

She is a monk in isolation – the entirety of her world confined to *The Narrator*, her room and the narrow streets leading from one to the other. Days and nights meld together; the indigo of the dawn seeping into the ochre of twilight. She experiences the passing of days like one watches a plant grow – it is a sapling one day, a towering behemoth the next. The day she misses Richa at the typesetter's is the day she first notices the girth of the tree of solitude that has spread.

When she first arrived in the city, in her days of walking behind the girls of her university in withdrawn and resigned companionship, the sapling was no bigger than the size of her thumb. The girls were nice, matronly in their affection towards their friend who carried a cloud of melancholy with her. The seed sown in childhood was just beginning to take root. They lent her their clothes when they found a week had passed without her noticing. They brought her food when she remained in bed, letting the light of the hours stamp its ephemeral marks on her. They held her hand and lifted her from the bed to take her to the cinema when she hadn't left her room in months. The girls were young, carrying their own burdens, but perhaps learned in the ways of repression and forgiveness. When they huddled around her late in the day, they shared giggles and details of their romantic exploits – stolen kisses, gaudy fur toys, billets-doux that made their toes curl.

Moments of nocturnal gatherings were eventually abandoned for clandestine rendezvous with lovers. The boys were no older than them but they showered wanton promises of eternal care and safety. She noticed their absence when it was time to leave, and the sapling sprouted leaves from its tender and pliable stem. A few years later, she would meet one of them in the market.

Her friend is with two little girls, the strain of their nurturing showing in the protruding folds of her stomach. 'I thought you would have found someone by now,' the woman says, hoisting her little girl higher on her shoulders while pulling back the older one, who constantly threatens to jump into the busy street, unwary of the passing vehicles. She is oddly familiar with her way of talking, even though ten years separate their first and current meeting. She knows that the mother means to express sympathy and concern, but she has no comforting words to provide to her in return. The mother juts out a lip and she wishes that her friend from yore would invite her to her home to give her a new sense of intimacy in the years when most recede into the filial warmth of their hearths. But the mother perhaps does not have the heart to reach out to someone whose presence could strip down mountains with its solemnity. There is only more sympathy and a pat on the arm, which is meant to be reassuring, but only stings the back of her eyes.

✿

On this day of shifted fate, an evening engagement weighs heavily on her head. Through the winding way out of the streets of the hidden watering hole of pedantic discourse that is *The Narrator*, on the ramshackle rickshaw driven by a salt-

and-pepper-haired ancient puller, and through more serpentine narrow lanes that are home as much to children squatting bare-bottomed by the drains as it is to their myriad of domesticated four-legged companions, she seethes at the invitation.

These gatherings are rare. Kumar – the editor-in-chief for two years – is loath to bring the cogs of *The Narrator* into his home. Class pretensions, which were previously expected to simply erase themselves under Chief's inerudite gaze, are now once again hoisted onto the pedestal that keeps Kumar on his throne. It is some nascent sense of association that impels Kumar to come forth with these invitations – and what invitations they are; merely passing remarks as the blue doors of the office close behind him.

Kumar has built a reputation in the small world of art for frequent flamboyant displays of his reach. While Chief had preferred the company of a few masters who could dazzle and blind with their worldly knowledge – looking down upon those denizens who hadn't reached such pinnacles yet – Kumar collects people who keep him within a hand's reach from fame. His – or rather, his secretary Poonam's – handwritten notes are grabbed from mailboxes with frothing glee by writers and painters, starlets and sculptors. Understandably, Jagannath's large belly, always peeking out from between the buttons of his shirt, and her sombre mien, like wilting leaves, are not necessarily expected at make an appearance.

But the invitations are extended nonetheless. The walls that were erected in the middle of the small office space of *The Narrator* could only be done by bringing down some others. Chief's outward display of camaraderie towards those who wore rayon instead of organza was a garb for the inward distance he sensed from them. The name of his family is one commonly prefixed with words like 'splendorous', 'august', 'celebrated'. Chief's colossal Rolls-Royce trundled lazily through the narrow alley of *The Narrator*, displacing the lines of vegetable vendors and their quadra- and bipedal customers, who had already started conducting their business. A man in a turban and starched white coat opened the car door for Chief, who walked in briskly without looking back. Mahesh, the young new writer, shares a two-bedroom flat with seven other men. Jagannath travels forty-five minutes to work – two buses, one overflowing jeep and fifteen minutes on foot. Kavita, though of a better standing, had only an Ambassador to drop her at the mouth of the street.

Three days after Chief's death, Kumar ceases to enact the role of a son of diamond traders, who is 'just like others'. He is several rungs higher in truth, looking down at the small men who dance at his command, and prefers to display the contrast in all its garishness. Around the Italian teak royal monstrosity that Chief used as a desk – where he was found a day after his death – Kumar builds his office. The *roshandans* are replaced with skylights that make the lizards on the walls glow with a heavenly ethereal light. The desks in the office are spread farther apart so that Kumar doesn't have to look at every face at all times. Tea and samosas are no longer allowed at *The Narrator*, and lunches and dinners are expected to be disregarded for the benefit of the magazine. Tactless pats on the back and boisterous laughs give way to persistent scowls and dour stares.

✿

Over the day's invitation, she prefers the roving eyes of her colleagues that pass over her face as if she is a ghost they have simply become at home with. The copies are corrected and proofs laid on their desks by hands that may or may not exist. Apart from Richa, sequestered in the dank corner of the typesetter's office, she fails to leave a lasting impression; those days under Chief's command when she could speak through her few words are quickly forgotten in the rubble that gathers when Kumar raises his office from his father's ashes, and the rearrangement of duties that corner the women so fast that most leave in fear of the downfall of their short-lived careers.

She alone persists. She is familiar with the smell of each inch of the office and its *vastu* design – northeast placement of the door, the south end that stinks with the pungent effluvia and fumes of the memories of a tobacco warehouse, the west wall that is covered with newspaper posters of Ganesh, Durga, Parvati, Shankar and thirty other deities; some of each. There is a dejected comfort in the history of its people and objects – in the representatives of five elements bundled together by Kumar's office from when Chief had first heard of Feng Shui; in the dent on Prabhakar's table where Kumar had thrown a paperweight; in the shape of the small cushion on her seat that engulfs her in a disquieting embrace for many hours. She could go, but she tires easily, and in the grinding routine that leaves her with little memory of the day, many years pass.

Her taciturnity is taken as a mark of her inferior faculties and, as is the fate of those of few words, her presence becomes simply tolerable – to be ignored and eventually omitted from matters of the workplace. It is a surprise then when Kumar, standing with a hand on the doorknob of his office and not

The Narrator, hastily announces their mandatory presence at the gathering at his bungalow later in the day. In a rare moment of formal kinship, her confusion is echoed by others. There is a brief silence in which Kumar remains unaffected, his stance at the door unchanging and expressions so fixed that she fears they will stay so forever. When, finally, the usual flurry of the office rises to its familiar crescendo, Kumar points an aggressive finger in her direction and turns back to take his place behind the mountains of periodicals raised on his desk.

She finds Mrs Pradhan standing with her hands pressed on the accordion gates to her house. Their neighbour, Sarita, is red-eyed and moving her hands as if wringing out her husband's laundry. He is a wife-beater, as frequent in his violent admonitions of her as he is religious in his participation in the state's growing anti-alcohol sentiments. 'It is the root of all evil, these foreign bad habits,' he once explained to her. It had only been a few days since she had moved into Mrs Pradhan's house. There were still some words in her, and the husband admired her close-lipped reticence over his wife's volubility, which was especially evident when he dragged her onto the street in rage.

With time, her attractive shyness became pomposity – 'these educated girls think they are better' – followed by a prudishness that was discussed widely among the young married men of the neighbourhood – 'that English-mumbling whore' – and finally, the advances she had been receiving unawares were simply forgotten. The suspicion the wives felt was replaced with a satisfactory pity for the girl, who, though well into her womanhood now, was unwanted, uncared for and unloved. They tutted and turned their heads to watch her leave for work every morning, shaking their heads at the ill luck that must taint the charts of a girl to have to fend for herself. They counted their lucky stars and, to the food they offered to the gods in their shrines, they added a redder apple and a spotless banana along with the roti dripping with ghee and the *sabzi* swimming in it. Sure, their husbands took their belts to them at times and were particularly disinterested in making the moments of their intimacy painless and comfortable, but at least they all had one.

Mrs Pradhan alone extends a helpful hand, however inadequate. She is widowed and childless. In this home full of conspicuous latticed windows and open, scalable courtyards, she is a woman freed from the dreaded expectations that should have started weighing her tenant down many years back. The two women, separated in age by three decades, are companionable. Mrs Pradhan is severe and perhaps even prudent. Nonetheless, she has warmed up to the younger woman.

It isn't particularly her kindness that makes her wrinkled face stretch into a smile every time the girl returns from work or the few times a day when she leaves her room. The truth is Mrs Pradhan's childlessness is undignified. She had been a good daughter. She had served her father and brothers with her own hands. She had lit the *chulha* with her nimble and soft hands until they were calloused. She had married the man who was picked out for her. It was a shame they had borne together for the few years he lived – she answering questions from distant relatives and passing neighbours, taking their remedies and advice without a stitch in her brows, and he complaining of his wife's barren womb over a game of cards and cigarettes with his old friends. For several years after he passed, her sorrow was much pitied. To have lost a husband so young was a tragedy, but to have lost him without birthing his children was a curse that not even gods could undo.

Mrs Pradhan, however, was not much interested. To Lord Krishna, who mutely witnessed her days from the wall where he remained untouched for decades, she sometimes said a silent prayer: 'Thank you for taking him when you did'.

Now in her sixth decade, her joints creak and her muscles ache. When she attempts to rise from the ground, she bends perpendicularly at her waist and stays so for several minutes before she can straighten herself. Once, she finds the pain in her back to be so severe that she chooses to relieve herself in her bed. She finds Mrs Pradhan teary-eyed and distressed. No words are exchanged, and in those few moments of silence – between the tired hush of nocturnal birds and the alarm of the morning ones, when crepuscular creatures stealthily go about their day – she helps Mrs Pradhan off the bed and cleans her.

She recognizes Mrs Pradhan's benevolence for what it is. Her silent endurance of her landlady's exploitation is measured. Her worrisome days are somewhat eased by the knowledge that the two women have created a symbiotic relationship. Her heaving sighs of relief on finding Mrs Pradhan intact after falls on slippery floors are not so much out of love but rather from the comfort of having secured another day of relative welfare.

In the solitude of her room, she worries that her existence has become like flotsam – discarded by the silent and invisible hands that caress and soothe the lives of others. Those wands and strings that ease the passage of time every once in a while have forgotten her. Mrs Pradhan, for now, keeps her from sinking. She is afraid of desiccating alone in the immensity of time. Mrs Pradhan's conviviality grows from the same place, if not worse.

At the entrance, Mrs Pradhan quickly shoos Sarita away and presses her large body to the doorframe to let her tenant pass.

She listens to the piercing sounds of the gate sliding shut and waits for the few words she must exchange with Mrs Pradhan to maintain the façade that both are afraid to break.

'Poor woman,' Mrs Pradhan mumbles. The women do not care much for Sarita's fate. In the last five years, she has become used to the sounds of thrashing and wailing that are commonplace in the neighbourhood. Each woman is privy to the wounds of the others, but none ever recognizes the bruises for what they are. A fall, a rash, an infection. At the vegetable vendor, at the crowded grocery store, in line to buy movie tickets, during Johny's chivalrous rescue of a damsel – lies are exchanged as cheap truths.

But she asks, 'Did he do it again?'

'Of course he did!' says Mrs Pradhan. She plonks heavily into her rocking chair, which stumbles with the weight. 'He is a beast. Angry at everything.'

What must enrage a man so much? she wonders. Chief was one of silent passions. He seethed at unseeable affronts, pushing *The Narrator* into progressively unmanageable disarray. His anger, however, was endurable. It waned and waxed like the moon, as *The Narrator*'s men never failed to notice. But Kumar wore his fury like a badge of honour. On the tip of his tongue and on his sleeve, like young lovers wear their hearts. Paperweights, magazines, pens and pencils, boxes of typewriter ribbons, slippers, shoes often flew through the air like motes of dust. His perpetual annoyance birthed a vicious frustration. Boys at tea stalls were smacked in the head for boiling the tea too hot. *Halwais* were yelled at and abuses were thrown at every unsuspecting passerby and rickshaw-puller.

Kumar's inability to control what crawled and lurked on the surface never bothered her too much. It was hysterical and childlike – a man showing his immaturity with the most infantile expressions of tantrums. Poonam, Kumar's secretary, was even more unbothered. No projectile could make her raise her eyes from her work.

'Maybe we should send him to Karim Chacha. See if he can grind the flour better than his bullocks,' she says. Mrs Pradhan chuckles but does not comment further. She knows when Mrs Pradhan wishes to be left alone. Among the various masks they wear, hers is expected to be blind. She frequently walks into Mrs Pradhan sprawled on the rocking chair with a profound blankness that would have filled her with fear if she didn't know of the copious amounts of opium the latter was in the habit of consuming.

Now she looks at the large frame of the woman, the dark spots of sweat seeping from under her arms and towards her breasts, and the avoidant downturn of her eyes. If she squints long enough, Mrs Pradhan could be her mother.

'I might get late today,' she says. 'Office party.'

When she nears the stairs to the first floor, she thinks she hears Mrs Pradhan mumble something about friends, and keeps walking.

FOUR

Mrs Pradhan is ill-disposed to accept that she is envious of her. At fifty-seven, her skin is like the pages of a book left on the windowsill in a rainstorm. Every year, there are new sheafs, and though she now takes no notice of the passage of time, the prime of her life seems farther away than it should be.

Her young tenant, by all standards, is past those youthful years as well. She has a few stiff, conspicuous strands of grey hair at her temples. A mother, a friend or a sister would have plucked them off her scalp, if the tenant had any. In five years, none have visited. Mrs Pradhan wishes to intrude – to one day stick an aching leg between the doors to her room and enquire about her activities. It is unusually incomprehensible that the young woman must spend her days in such seclusion. In her stupors, she often dreams that within the four walls of the room that she rents, there is a boisterous life – suspenseful, dangerous – that Mrs Pradhan is not aware of. She wears a lacy dress like that dark-haired woman in last year's spy movie. She carries a gun – or only a small thumb-sized imitation of it – and turns the tides of the city's governance.

But she is no one. There is no bubbling genius in her isolation. There is no evidence of a passion that so often afflicts those of an intellectual and obsessive temperament. She is ordinary, even less than mediocre. She looks like the million others of the city flitting back and forth from work, bent over the day's newspaper but only vaguely remembering the events of the world beyond their desks and documents. As far as Mrs Pradhan understands, she is not of much importance at her work either. Besides the few times three years ago, when her name appeared in hidden corners of the magazine's volumes, she is already lost to posterity like a fossil.

Mrs Pradhan is, however, envious of the time she has; of the nimble body that could hurry when it needed to; of a mind not enslaved and slowed by earthly dependencies. Her own limbs are as thin as the growing twigs on the crown of a young tree, while her joints are inflamed and swollen. They creak like old, unoiled doors and throb when the rest of her only hopes to relax. Mrs Pradhan refuses to look at her fingers, knobby and ugly like leguminous roots. On cold days, her mind refuses to lift the body it is supposed to command, and she lies in her bed, grinding her teeth at her misfortunes, hoping that her young tenant would come find her on her perfectly functional legs.

Her body refuses to remember, but she recalls those stolen moments behind fallen walls. When elders gathered in halls and rooms to share, in fearful delight, the day's rumours and gossips on the fate of their country – perhaps to be divided – Mrs Pradhan snuck away from home and into the arms of her lovers. The young men trembled and groaned, not so much from desire than fear for their reputations. Fathers are brutal in their violence and stubborn in decreeing consequences. The girl who will become Mrs Pradhan takes little occupation in their minds. She is warm and fragile, and what might befall her is lost somewhere in her flesh. She herself only knows the demands of her body, and amid the fear that has gripped the nation, the smidgen of insulation that came from families occupied in getting their affairs in order, she found she could satiate those demands with frivolous boys.

As she lifts a fresh betel leaf and runs her painful fingers over its smooth surface, as she adds a thick sludge of lime and a dollop of *gulkand* at its centre, as she tucks away a dark pellet under the other accoutrements, she remembers.

Who Mrs Pradhan was before she became Mrs Damodar Pradhan is no longer important. The pigtailed girls of her childhood, the stripling young men of her new youth, and the faces of her mother, father and sisters – never seen again after a border split the country in two – are now forgotten. She recalls the image of a chubby daughter of an attorney who played the role of a husband so well she would stuff a piece of cloth down her skirt, and another of a boy, no older than her, with skin so white it seemed to reflect the rays of the sun. She never heard of the girl again, but the boy was said to have died in the riots in Benaras a few years after she was married.

She never sees Damodar before marrying him. At twenty, she is old and her prospects recede like the neap tides. Her father tucks himself into a cane chair in his small office, and her mother beats her chest, wailing loudly enough to invite the burning queries of neighbours. But such is the fate of a girl past her prime.

She finds Damodar to be a regular man. He has two eyes, a nose, a set of lips, all ten fingers, likely all ten toes, two hands, two legs, two ears, one torso. There is nothing unusual about him, and when he speaks, it is with the poise and assurance of a university-educated man. His voice is deep and clear; there are no shakes in his grip when he pours ghee into the fire. He does not have the nervous tics of a timid man, nor does he carry himself with any pride.

Damodar inherits a house in the crowded streets of the old city. Each house rests shoulder to shoulder with the next. The doors are not locked – some don't even have doors, just a curtain screening marital occupations from passersby. Mrs Pradhan is no stranger to the needs of the flesh, but the passions of the relatively destitute still draw colour to her cheeks. From the outside, lined with broken latticed windows and a corrugated steel door, the Pradhans' new residence has the same impoverished appearance as the lower classes they now find themselves regrettably among.

Mrs Pradhan, however, is told to trust her husband, and when the accordion doors are slid open and the small passageway covered, the length and breadth of their dwelling take her by surprise. Mrs Pradhan plants a ceremonial tulsi in the centre of the courtyard and initiates her domestic life by placing a small statue of Krishna in the small ala overlooking it.

Mr and Mrs Pradhan do not consummate their marriage in the first year. Nor the second and third. Or the fourth. By the fifth, she finally discerns her father's brooding retreat into his office and her mother's screeching wails. By the sixth, she curses her long-neglected family for her circumstances. The only consolation of her nuptials had been the frequent accessibility of those relished moments of her youth.

It is difficult to say if Damodar Pradhan was simply of discrete inclinations, or if he preferred the company of others. In the seventh year of their marriage, Mrs Pradhan, determined to take what she believes must rightfully belong to her in return for the labour she provides to Mr Pradhan's household, decides to take matters into her own hands.

Damodar is a stoic man. He is grateful for Mrs Pradhan's company and for the pristine state she keeps their house in. He is not a busy man. The nature of his work pushes him to return home often, and he fills his time with literature. He fancies himself a polymath and indulges heavily in Robert Abernathy and Poul Anderson. In the story of Danny and of Danny's friends and of Danny's house, he finds no joy. But he has heard of *Tortilla Flat* and Steinbeck, and in the remaining time, he prefers the works of fantastical imaginations.

These interests are to mask the failings of his body. With his literary proclivities, he hopes that he is considered a man of unusual intellect. When he gathers with his friends for glasses of local madeira, he quietens. They are braggarts and crass in the details of their sexual exploits. His silence only fires curiosity and dies only with his angry complaints of Mrs Pradhan's barrenness. Flowery enough to satiate his drunken companions, and vague enough not to betray his inexperience. He pushes the conversations till they take on more gentlemanly tones of discourse. It is a different, albeit difficult matter that he curls up into his cocoon when they talk of Gandhi's treatises and Bose's failures. At least, he avoids the other discussions.

Mrs Pradhan ultimately gathers the courage to confront her husband. At nights, she remembers those few encounters before her marriage and weeps. Here is a man who lies beside her but remains as strange as on the day they met. She feels functional and discarded, a machine or a mere helper in the home of the Pradhans. Outside his office, in which he reclines in his rocking chair with a tattered book held close to his eyes, she worries at her sari and swallows from her dry mouth. Her courage lasts only so long – explosive and loud – until Mr Pradhan's eyes, first widen in shock, lower and rise again, red with disbelief. He is first angry, then incensed, and finally so furious that his legs and hands shake. Mrs Pradhan flinches and recedes, and never brings it up again. The anger too is a mask.

For many months, Mrs Pradhan does not know what Mr Pradhan does for a living. On every first Monday, he hands her a slip with a number and a cheque. In the village where she grew up, there were no banks. Until the moment she receives the first cheque from Damodar, she is not sure how a bank works or what one must do to be affiliated with one. Her family was never in need of such financial institutions. Her father's prestigious position as a small-time professor in a fledgling university was only enough to get them through the months.

Her mother, however, had a small *tijori* which she kept hidden in the deep corners under her bed. Several other *petis* of her marriage trousseau and some flimsy cardboard boxes of clutter were pushed into the remaining spaces to make it unattractive to any living creatures, besides rats. Mrs Pradhan was shown the contents of the box for the first time a day before her wedding – a couple of gold *kangans*, one silver nutcracker studded with rubies and emeralds, and a pair of gold-plated heavy earrings were handed to her. She had never known that they were in possession of such riches and the treasure in her palms felt dirty and dishonest. Her mother had whispered never to tell her husband about them and to always keep them hidden from the 'follies of men'.

For three weeks, Mrs Pradhan waits for Damodar to enquire after the slips of paper. Though he gives her no reason to fear him, as impassive as he tends to be, Mrs Pradhan is concerned that a display of such ignorance might lower her in the eyes of her husband. She is not aware that Damodar does not think much of her anyway, and for one more week, until the arrival of another cheque, she spends her hours in a state of such unease that she develops a stomachache.

It is only when the last annas jingle in the tin jar she found filled with coins and paper money on the first day, that she realizes where more would come from. The next morning, she waits for Damodar to leave for work and hailing down a rickshaw by belting towards a salt-and-pepper-haired puller, she learns the tiresome ways of the bank. Damodar never realizes her struggle but is always surprised at her growing capabilities; nor does he ever fail to boast about the role of his liberal support in her expanding practical education.

Damodar is a newsreader for the Indian State Broadcasting Service and, for a brief time, at the newly rechristened All India Radio. His faceless voice becomes the chosen and cherished one for the few prosperous in the city, and at small gathering houses and shops that serve as elementary salons. He speaks with confidence and conviction – the news of the autonomy of Bengal and Orissa, of Nehru's prime ministership, and the war that ravages the people ravaging his people. In his deep voice and refined articulation, he speaks of the new constitution and its implications, of riots in Bombay and their implications, of laws and articles and speeches and their implications – all of which he himself fails to understand.

But the very rasp of his voice, which has people pressing their ears to the radio, honed and evolving over time, is now spreading roots of sickness deep into the tender flesh of his lungs. Neither he nor his evening companions, with whom he spends time in underground clubs stinking with tendrils of grey smoke concealing the sharpness of their faces, notice the thinning forearms or the clothes that seem to hang loosely over his frame.

Mrs Pradhan, however, sees. She is aware of his lack of appetite and the new tremors in his previously assured hands; of the shadows under his eyes and the dark, distant gaze that appears when he attempts to read his much-treasured foreign novels. Mrs Pradhan is uneducated, unbothered and distinctly uncared for, and the night she finds him stiff in his office, she exhales a breath of bone-chilling relief before letting out a blood-curdling scream to curry the pity and assistance of her neighbours.

✿

Widowed, Mrs Pradhan finds a peculiar, rather tingling joy in her new solitude. After Mr Pradhan is cremated and she has spent several days in mourning and further garnering – even squeezing – the sympathy of others, she wakes up one day well after the morning hours. The sun is almost overhead, throwing the courtyard into a dazzling display of the shadows of the neem that grows in one corner. She does not wrap her previous day's sari around her undressed body. A breeze filters in through the latticed windows, and she raises the end of her petticoat to feel the breeze on her knees and shins for the first time since she was a frock-donning child.

Without bathing, she plucks a leaf from the tulsi she planted almost six years ago. She joins her hands at the idol of Krishna, which she has cleaned and polished every day, but does not say a prayer. Instead of the dusty and suffocating cooking room, she drags the small *chulha* into the courtyard. The fire kindles and dances in the autumn breeze, and when she drops the leaf into the tea, it sizzles with a new exuberance.

Mrs Pradhan finds that a widow – and a widow at less than thirty years of age – is a sight to be pitied. She is burdened with a life of bad fortune. Her charts are not in her favour. A distant cousin of Damodar brings a palm reader to tell if it is the sins of her past lives that have brought her such sorrow. A *havan* is conducted to ward off the evil that a pundit sees with his third eye. Mrs Pradhan sits through them, first numb, then gleeful. When people leave, they press money into her hands.

It is the first time she realizes that she must soon fend for herself, but for over five years, she has saved and thrifted. Damodar was a man of no needs besides his books with green creatures and beasts on them, and Mrs Pradhan was unsure of what lay in the depths of the ancient city that she could amuse herself with.

The visitors are an ocean, then a stream, and one day no more than the trickle of sewer water that swims in the thin drains around her house. She counts enough money to get her through a year. She will think of her circumstances when she is halfway through. Her charts, she finds, are not as misaligned as commiserating and whispering cousins and neighbours claim. Her Saturn is in the seventh house, Mercury in conjunction.

Young men flow into the city like a swarm of locusts. A neophyte of a government has taken root and administration, governance, bureaucracy have opened to the people of the nation. While people take cover in fear of the young blood that takes to the streets and brandishes *lathis* in generational rage, Mrs Pradhan opens the doors of her establishment with its many rooms to them. Her widowhood takes precedence – her tragedy and the adversity of her situation so pathetic in the eyes of others that it washes over her youth.

Once again, Mrs Pradhan finds herself in the company of striplings. The four rooms on the first floor and the two below – including her husband's beloved office with hundreds of books – are opened to the tenants. Mrs Pradhan is careful, pushing and prodding at the inclinations and impulses of only one tenant at a time. The rest become like her sons – fed twice a day, provided with boiling water in the winters and occasionally cared for during illnesses and injuries. Her room becomes her passionate sanctuary. Stealing steps over the gallery late in the night swell her chest with giddiness. Mrs Pradhan seizes the freedom Damodar once denied her.

✿

Age eventually does catch up with Mrs Pradhan. She becomes Bhabhi, then Behenji, and one day Mataji. She sits on her husband's rocking chair in the gallery, overlooking the giant neem, and through the latticed windows watches the street bustle with the mundanity of hundreds. She remembers Damodar Pradhan, who would spend several hours in his study in this same chair, reading tales of zapping ships and malformed babies. He had complained of poor eyesight once. *I should have insisted he go to a doctor*, thinks Mrs Pradhan.

But it isn't just age that leaves her with a trickling of tenants. In those years after Damodar's death, she rarely steps beyond her street. The young men bring her groceries and household supplies without needing to be told. They sometimes clean and wash the courtyard, and she admires them from the rocking chair. At night, she gives in to the demands of her body and those of her ephemeral lovers. Except for one, she never hears from them again. They burn with a different passion and take to the streets to shout slogans. Sometimes they come home bloodied, not having made it as far as they wished before the lathis rained down on them.

Sounds of spirited nights are replaced by those of distant gunshots and occasional screaming. Sometimes, she hears the neighbours' radio blast off in the quiet of the night, and the news of wars fills her dreams. The boys don't always return home. She listens for those squeaking steps that used to set her heart ablaze, but only hears the cries of jackals calling to each other.

She does not yet resent the passage of time. When she is breathing her last, she will remember the names of her young lovers. She will remember the working-class torso of a farmer in search of a city job, the coal-like skin of a writer who cried throughout the night, the pigmented lips of a young newspaper publisher who would guiltily and hurriedly snatch the *Gita* before he had even tied his pajamas around his waist.

By the time the boys start returning and renting rooms for longer than a few months at a time, she does not feel so agile anymore. They are young too. Still adolescent. *If I had children when I was married, they would be this age*, she tells herself. They join their hands in front of her and politely ask for water. They hand her their rent in small envelopes that they hold with both their hands. They sweep the courtyard on their days off from work.

She hires a woman to clean and cook when the thin knuckles of her fingers start stiffening. They become gnarly and ugly, and one day when she lifts her sari, she is appalled at the grotesque shape that stares back at her. A *vaidya* advises her to take some opium. Now, as she watches the woman sweep the courtyard, it is with the distant gaze of one abandoning the humdrum of the present for the vivid souvenirs of yesterday.

✿

Perhaps she too has given herself to an existence that is not fast-rooted in the present, Mrs Pradhan thinks. But for the time spent talking to the women of the neighbourhood and in devoted exultation from her medication, the years have flowed into each other. Mrs Pradhan couldn't really tell what happened the year before, or the year before that. But those spent before and after Damodar Pradhan were still intoxicating in memory. The blurred recollections of nights long past still set her stomach aching with senile butterflies.

Her gauche tenant might be plain – unmanaged frizzy hair tied in a bun, shabby *salwar kameez* and rounded shoulders – but was Mrs Pradhan much different from her? She uncovers her gilded box. The shine of the silver nutcracker beckons her to prepare another paan. *Where else could she bury her long days*, she sighs, and cracks with its sharp teeth another supari.

FIVE

A lamp on the gate pillar of Kumar's house is broken. Its pentagonal frame hangs dangerously from its base, one glass shade lost, leaving her in shadows where she stands. The security guard squints and peers at her through the bars of the corrugated structure. His thick white moustache quivers from the strain of first seeing and then placing her face.

She has arrived in a rickshaw and then on foot. The scenery changes from the narrow, crowded streets of her neighbourhood to the bustling industrial spectacle where iron bars are hawked next to an incinerating pile of acrid waste, beside defecating masses squatting on an open ground, watching the evening trains pass by. The puller sighs with relief when a turn leads to a wider, less-crowded road. The rickshaw flies easily over the wide asphalt stretch, the few cars and buses far and between. Since she began working at *The Narrator*, she has had little reason to come to this part of the city, where a college friend had once resided with her splendorous grandparents. Now, she doesn't know anyone of such prodigal ancestry – and if, in her ignorance, she does, she isn't aware of it. Under the last dimming sun, the boulevards, littered with fallen blooms of gulmohar, engulf each passing vehicle in their vastness before the streetlights blink to life in her wake.

In the quiet, green neighbourhood of Kumar's, she is embarrassed of her shabbiness. The bright pink and yellow of her salwar kameez are loud and screaming in their cheapness. The synthetic fabric rustles and susurrates unseemly with every movement. The rickshaw puller hums a song in his local tongue, and she asks him to drop her at the side of the road. An Impala blinds her momentarily and she miscounts the money she hands the puller. Under the imagined scrutiny of the driver, she wants immediate distance from her rackety rickshaw. She hands him five coins and hurries away. The puller, smiling at his luck and smirking at women's foolishness, touches the money to his forehead and turns around.

At Kumar's door, she recognizes the expression of disdain on the guard's face. His standing in Kumar's world is not much different from her own bizarre presence at the mouth of this mansion, but he only ever salutes the metal boxes of imported cars and the unseeing eyes of the affluent. There is no familiarity in her eyes that instead of looking away with the expectant obedience of class, simply stare into his own as if asking *what next?* A horn blares at them both. The guard hurriedly lifts the latch of the gate and opens it wide for a Mercedes. He stands in military salute until the car disappears into the driveway. She passes through the gate, which the guard leaves to swing shut behind her. It is the only courtesy he will allow someone who arrived on their own two legs.

✿

A quarter of an hour later, the generous displays of opulence have already lost their novelty. The garden fountain that had previously charmed her now appears to be clogged. The cherub's penis sputters; the uneven stream splatters on silk saris and Italian suits, and into glasses of rum and Coke. A group of musicians replace guests by the fountain to smoke between accented renditions of Western songs and bad imitations of Bollywood music. The basin is soon littered with Pall Mall filters.

She trails behind Poonam, who has brought her fiancé with her. He is a beautiful man by all standards. His shoulders flare out from the thinner contours of his waist and torso, his legs uninterrupted in pleated black pants. He has a rich crop of hair and a trace of beard that wafts a breeze of Old Spice. Poonam calls him Mahir. She believes it only to be an endearing moniker, accompanied as that introduction is with a roguish smile. Mahir does not correct her.

She is aware of Poonam's charm through quiet observation of the secretary at *The Narrator*. Poonam arrives a few days after Chief's death and begins working as Kumar's secretary, replacing a matronly Kavita. She, however, does not have the same reservedness as the woman she has ousted – the last living memory of Chief's leadership. Poonam is flamboyant in her demands, so undisguised and garrulous in the insistence of her importance that, in a rare turn of events, *The Narrator* becomes incapable of functioning without her. Poonam, in her own words, is as ambitious as a crocodile hitchhiking to the beach to embrace a larger world. She admires Poonam's conviction but does not relay to her what she knows of those creatures.

Poonam and Mahir introduce themselves to every guest – she, a budding journalist with an interest in international relations;

he, a government officer in the railways. The details of their occupation change and form with the needs of the moment. Poonam is never simply a secretary; her role swells and, though it never reaches the heights that Chief habitually claimed for himself, it is never too far from the responsibilities of Kumar, and never close enough to her reality. Mahir is sometimes a chief engineer, once a deputy divisional railway manager, and to an air force commander, a principal chief personnel officer. Truth is lost in the fiction that Poonam and Mahir knit for their gains and the entertainment of others. She, on the other hand, holds the chafing material of her salwar kameez close to herself, the sound of synthetic rubbing against synthetic so subdued that neither Poonam nor Mahir pay any mind to the shadow that dogs them. She is rather glad of it too. She is only vaguely familiar with the faces of Kumar's guests. They reside in the subconscious pools of her sensory vastness, but she does not know which billboard or magazine they are from.

When Poonam and Mahir briefly tire of vicariously hosting, perhaps looking for opportunities that might break the shackles of their lives, which they distantly know will remain bound in their middle-class realities; they instead whisper amongst themselves about the scandalous lives of those gathered. Kumar himself remains seated in the living room beyond a glass wall, several of his guests hanging on to his every word as though he is quoting scripture, and averts his gaze from where *The Narrator* now stands in a group, cowed by the displays of wealth on both person and stone.

A writer, recently awarded the Literary Academy award, and his wife walk past their unacknowledged group. 'But she's not the one he was photographed with, is she?' mumbles Poonam.

They turn their heads to follow the demure movements of the writer's companion. Jagannath sniffs at his glass of rum, the idea for a scandalous exposé already taking form in his head. It wouldn't be the first, and before *The Narrator* runs to the ground, it won't be the last. Jagannath has followed the writer through tabloids and newspapers, the radio and the TV, for years. He is loath to read too often, but when he does, he expects the earth to move from under his feet and for the world to burst into an explosion of yet unseen colours. When he picks the writer's most celebrated works, he is disappointed. It is basic. Uninspiring.

The obsession takes hold – first through word of mouth, then breathless consumption of any detail about the man. *How could a man of such middling talents command such respect and devotion?* Jagannath thinks. For his own investigation – one he believes will catapult him into new horizons, appease his wife, shower him with wealth and finally drag him into sobriety – he tails the writer to hotel lobbies and private parties. All for his craft to lay bare the craft of another.

Jagannath is not alone in his desire for closeness to the people who now surround their small, invisible group. For years, each has become a silent spectator of someone or the other in the garden. A dangerously thin actress, perpetually unblinking, recently returned from America after her first role in a Hollywood film. A textile mogul caught in a scam for annexing the land of farmers – Kumar threw Mahesh's article on this into the garbage bin. A young man, recently instated as the chief in his father's stead, suspected of being involved in his father's freak accident in a helicopter. A lawyer accused of arson. A sculptor enmeshed in a prostitution ring. A singer caught smuggling cocaine across borders. An industrialist seducing a godwoman. A rising filmmaker, now revered and awarded in the country, for being one of the first to be mentioned in the same breath as Mulligan and Mankiewicz and Lean.

✿

It is at Aarav's behest that the shamefully plebeian aspects of Kumar's life find themselves breathing the same air as celebrated literary giants and sparkling icons of art. He is Kumar's school friend, his dorm mate from the time they nursed split palms and sore bottoms together after the Fathers at boarding school caught them in their harmless adolescent mischief. She recognizes him from the covers of the magazines he regularly graces. He is a connoisseur, an epicure, a critic. His movies play in theatres all around the world. Their cleaners and organizers can barely point out India on a map. The viewers jump to their feet and applaud the heart-wrenching but 'authentically marvellous display of the saddening poverty and division of the South'. Aarav's word on cinema is final – his approval of a commercial movie a cause for celebration; his disparaging remarks on the mainstream big screen a cause to shut studios. He is *'Le premier auteur de l'Inde'*, as one magazine puts it.

She finds him more politician than auteur. As he moves from Jagannath to Prakash, then Poonam, Mahir and Mahesh, shaking their one hand with both of his, he dons the smile of an MLA. It is suspicious and fixed, exuding a boyish charm in the fullness of teeth that it reveals. She watches for the corners to tremble in concealed agitation, but they never do. By the time it reaches her, she is unable to look anywhere else.

Aarav regales them with stories of Kumar's exploits at the boarding school in the mountains. She can barely imagine Kumar as a doddering teenager who had pined after the headmaster's daughter or almost set a room on fire in the days before the Diwali holidays. Kumar, perhaps fearful of his friend's good humour, joins them at the edge of the garden. Next to Aarav, it is hard to believe they are the same age. It is harder still to imagine that the two could share the kind of intimate bond that endures and thrives in the decades that pull people apart across several borders. Kumar's lips have begun their premature journey towards his chin. There are traces of emerging jowls; his thin hair exposes an unhealthy, inflamed scalp; the back of his hands are marked with liver spots. Aarav, on the other hand, stands as if slaving arms pull his shoulders towards the sky. The smooth skin of his cheeks is stretched snugly over the contours of his thin face. She catches Poonam roving her eyes over the details of his profile.

Aarav's stories, though progressively lewd, retain the charm of a master storyteller. In the swish of his hands and the suggestive rise of his eyebrows, in the pauses that leave them holding their breath and the inflections of his voice that startle and amaze, Aarav's standing in the world of cinema soon becomes obvious in the mesmerization that fixes on the listeners' faces as if set in wax or stone.

'Kumar and I briefly apprenticed at a newspaper together,' he says, his eyes roving over his friend's aghast face. Aarav chuckles to himself – perhaps amused at Kumar's discomfort or simply aware of the effect that the publicization of this story would have on him. 'There was a girl there ... what was her name, Kumar? Rupal?'

'Renuka,' Kumar whispers over the rim of his glass.

'Ah yes, Renuka!' Aarav claps his hands together. His eyes settle on her briefly, searching, rather curious. 'She looked like you,' he says, pointing a finger towards her face. He wears a silver ring on his index finger, the only jewellery on his person, not signifying an engagement; rather indicative of the lack of one. Under Aarav's favourable scrutiny, she feels stripped and naked, raw as if he will pluck her feared insecurities and exhibit them as oddities of comic characters in his films.

'Anyway' – a wave of his hand – 'Kumar was quite taken with her. He would arrange these beautiful getaways and evening rendezvous – roses and chocolates. Very romantic. Very unlike Kumar. I was quite surprised when you did not marry her. After the headmaster's daughter, it was the first time I had seen him this smitten. But I guess certain traditions must be held close to our hearts.'

Kumar, through this soliloquy, stands quiet, his glass drained of its rum till he is sipping at the last dregs of melting ice. He is not a ramrod man; since the day she arrived at the office, she has observed the mound under the back of his neck growing larger and larger until it blended into the curves of his shoulders. Perhaps he now grieves his past, reminded of a distant love that slipped from his fingers in fear of the standing and fortune that he wished to keep clutched in the palm of his hands. His back straightens, the jutting head pulled back till he towers over his conniving friend. It is a proud stance, illusory and fraudulent, as much to dispel queries from his underlings as to remind himself of the consequences of the comforts he had chosen.

Under Aarav's cordiality, there is a lurking, underhanded malignity. He picks and chooses his words with intention, meant to leave others silent and raw. She is uncommonly attracted to it, like children compelled to look at the desiccating corpse of a runover puppy on the road. She discards the company of Poonam and Mahir, trudging instead behind Aarav's cavalier back. What Poonam knows only as passing gossip – overheard from those who likely knew even less – Aarav details and paints as truth.

'The Hollywood-returned actress is a whore, potentially addicted to substances of the worst kind. She only got her role because she sold her body for it,' he says, his voice never betraying the lingering hurt he once received from her. The lawyer, caught amongst the mob he had once fought for and bankrupted from their demands, had indeed set his firm on fire to reclaim a fraction of his lost wealth through insurance. 'He is probably carrying some coke in his pocket right now,' Aarav says of the singer, and of the textile mogul: 'He does not even need that land. Power and greed are the most potent aphrodisiacs.'

Never once, in the throes of his condemnation of the company Kumar keeps, does Aarav betray astonishment at the shadow he has drawn, captivated. He has commanded attention of artists whose names become common knowledge, matters of discussion in homes where their works never reach, from countries most will never visit nor learn the nuances that propel a city or a country from a mere tourist attraction to a centre of existence and mundane routines.

An artist who toils for years alone, shunned for the impossibility of their undertaking and isolated to drown in the pool of their conscience from which comes their work, meets bewitched ears for the first time. He meets men whose creations he has absorbed and admired, emulated to show devotion through subtle nods in his own works – a reference in the pan of a camera or a line structured, words lifted and placed to evoke in the viewer the face of a master, the particular drape of a sari on an actress or a distant gaze caught at the end.

To behold the attention of his gods, he soon forgets the time when it had been only himself and the unsettling chatter in his mind. Aarav simply expects a trailing admirer – one he finds everywhere he goes.

✿

The memories and stories, experiences and histories – pain and joy – that make Aarav are perhaps not within the scope of our narration. It is rather difficult to grasp what makes a person the culmination of that which he presents to the world – utterly impossible to know the beginnings of that which he does not.

Biographies written decades later read superficially. His daughter – conceived in the cold winters of Bern with the same actress he had once branded a 'whore', whispered to a woman who faded from his memories like the wispy florets of dandelion caught in a breeze – calls him an 'enigma'.

'Whatever he wished to say, he said through his films. At home, he remained a mystery to me and my brother. To my mother, though married six years, he was rather like a reserved lover, denying her that constant and vexing companionship and humdrum conversations that mark the end of courtship and the beginning of marriage.'

Aarav, however, in that moment, when he and she walk towards a wallpaper depicting the expanse of the Valley of Flowers – as at odds with the Kishangarhi folding chairs as the chairs themselves are to the crystal decanter and glasses on a fleur-de-lis-carved wooden dumbwaiter – and for many years after, until in his eighties – his mind weakened with the weight of dozens of stories he no longer has time to tell – believes himself to be a victim. The woman herself never leaves the periphery of his thoughts, even when he offers to make her a drink that wouldn't taste of rum, which she detests, or when he invites her up to the room where Kumar has offered him boarding for the duration of his short visit to the city.

He remembers the day he received the call at school, followed by a car that was to drive him back to his hometown. His father, his greatest friend, is found dead in the early morning, leaving him and his younger brother in the care of his illiterate mother. In his father's study, one of Victorian splendour, complete and resplendent with golden-spined tomes of law and politick – some written by the man himself, radical and revolutionary – leather-backed chairs, globes, charts and maps, Aarav and his father had spent many evenings together.

His father did not have much love for his mother – a marriage of convenience arranged by his own father to secure the social standing he had lost post-Independence for printing diatribes in support of Hitler's genocide.

'The woman is as daft as a brush,' he would say, 'not even suited for the kitchen, where she might blow the servants into smithereens with some act of unimagined stupidity.'

Aarav is still young when he hears this, and as he grows older, his father's observations of his mother prove fairly true. His mother speaks no English, reads only novels – of lazy romances and indecorous romps. In the company of learned men, she laughs and declares she cannot tell the difference between sherry and wine. She confines herself to those interests that require no thinking, no logic, no reason – in short, the interests of women.

She rushes to the cinema to admire the brooding actors of her day, but has no appreciation for those finer details of theatre that elevate a narrative from a simple story onscreen to a masterpiece. She is a philistine, never read Mann or Rimbaud or Smith; never recognized Sargent or Rembrandt or Rubens. The father contemplates for many years the right words to describe her; words that would convey the lack of culture in her without filling his son with ideas that might affect his view of his own origins, and one day, giving up, he simply exclaims, 'She's so rural ... so Indian.'

But it is in the care of these tasteless bourgeoisie that Aarav, all of fifteen, and his brother find themselves. Men and women who sit, unbathed and odorous, outside Supreme Courts and the residences of lowly politicians to demand in their crass local tongues the institution of such hypothetical and metaphysical notions as equality and justice; abstract concepts that even Aarav's young brother understands to be futile in the face of reality – that power cannot exist without the powerless.

It is these thoughts that churn in his mind when he invites this woman into his room at Kumar's house. In his distraction, he barely remembers the words he says to her or what convinces her to join him – or if she simply follows him, compelled by some unfolding obsession. He distances himself from his mother's family, who spit on the politicians and businessmen who give him the green light to tell whichever stories he wants, wherever he wants. It is a rather different matter that often his grandfather's name – the one of the local tongue – opens doors for him that he wouldn't have known to knock on otherwise, or that his mother labours for his comforts in the days when unemployed and fantasizing, he spends a decade confined to his rooms, stoking his disdain for the woman who dispels all illusions of equality, and remembering his father with whom he could truly discuss the greater joys of life. He would have been proud of his success; his mother barely understands the significance of what he creates.

The woman in his room now is no different. In the bright colours of her clothes, he instantly senses an absence of finesse. Her short forehead, her sloping shoulders, her flabby arms, the squinting of her eyes with every sip of her rum, and her absolute inability to contribute to the conversation he has only half-heartedly tried to draw her into – she is a specimen of the same kind. He sees his mother. He is only vaguely aware of the resistance she puts up, slightly vexed by her unresponsive body. But, like others, the fight recedes soon enough.

SIX

Kumar, though unsympathetic, is not unaware of her. In his father's time at *The Narrator*, she was involved and active, even resourceful. She had a few informants who would occasionally show up in their tattered clothes carrying the odour of their stuffy lives that stuck and lingered. She had been quick to learn, and several times he would find her peering over his shoulders to absorb that which she did not feel too comfortable asking to be taught.

But Kumar is familiar with her type of melancholy. At *The Narrator*, dozens of desks and a glass wall separate him from the world. At home, there are servants who relay to other servants his needs and wants. Yet he does not live under a rock. He started as a political writer, and so often, politics was best rendered with threats to privacy and the autonomy of bodies. Women like her were not sickened as much by the cruelties of a raging man as they were by their own resultant rage that they had no one but themselves to inflict on. That fettered fury behind their eyes was common. Even characteristic. Many took to monkish silence like her, others to holding it close to their hearts to shoo away any who might come near. In another time and life, Kumar thinks, she could have been a stellar professional. But the stains of times gone erode her into early oblivion.

Since their boyhood days, when he and Aarav would smuggle clear bottles of home-brewed alcohol into their dorm room, Kumar has found that each morning after, he wakes with a peculiar worry. Aarav is as good a friend as any man in his early thirties can be – ready with promises of lending money; the greatest pledge of masculine friendship. The worry usually stems from his memories of the previous days. They are blurred and heavy, squeezed into distorted sounds and darkened edges with the numbness of alcohol. He remembers some derisive words here, an embarrassing story there; mentions of Renuka that he would rather erase, or affairs of his father that he pretends never existed to begin with.

Sometimes, he also remembers snippets that, by their very nature, seem of the kind that he wasn't necessarily supposed to witness. In earlier years, it was some powder dropped into a drink with a sleight of hand, or recently, coercive words that slowly lose their sweetness as the night passes. Kumar is not blind to Aarav's increasingly questionable patterns, the first signs of which emerged in the home of a whore picked from the streets of Sonagachi. It had seemed a great rite of passage, their farewell from the gates of a school leading into the darkened boudoir of a sex worker. It was a secret they had shared and then kept together. Aarav, like Kumar, had seemed plainly naïve and inexperienced – until his hand closed around the woman's throat.

Kumar had been perplexed, amused, and though loath to accept, aroused – all disappearing when the woman's thrashing subsided, her face pale and drained of colour, her crazed eyes half-closed. They had run out of the house without checking on her, forever left wondering about her undetermined fate; but while Kumar had been stunned and afraid, Aarav had simply panted for several minutes before exclaiming, 'We will remember this night forever.'

Aarav has the fallings and failings of a man, but regardless, Kumar believes he is a good man. Perhaps his manners towards women are not ideal – more reminiscent of his own father, Chief, than the clan of activists and former freedom fighters Aarav comes from. Moreover, the women never complain or inform anyone, so they must not mind awfully. Besides, whoever heard of an artist who does not have their own set of eccentricities and deep-rooted maleficence? On account of his art alone – one of its kind and unique enough to make waves where their nation is known only for its famines and dirty children – he could be forgiven his transgressions. Aarav is good to him too; he brought him supper when he was locked in their dorm room, incapacitated with blinding headaches; he had stood beside him like a brother at his father's cremation and Renuka's reception.

It is Aarav's nonchalance towards his own actions that truly worries him. Bogged down as he is with trying to remember those who were regaled with his adolescence, he does not notice Aarav in his office right away. Amidst the clutter of the room – the piles of foreign magazines that Chief had subscribed him to and Kumar finds himself unable to unsubscribe from, fluttering chalk dust under the fan, the moth-eaten old editions from his father's time – Aarav, in his *mulmul* kurta-pyjama, is laughable.

In his friend's face, he sees a semblance – an imitation – of remorse. It is unlike him to engage in small matters or comment on the apparent weather or fiddle with the pages of a magazine.

By the time Aarav makes the request he has come for, Kumar knows what it will be about. He had seen the two together the day before – her a trailing duckling behind a larger, guiding drake.

'I suppose she wouldn't care too much if you gave her career a little push. A little favour from me,' Aarav says before parting.

✿

The feigned remorse – or rather a feeble fear of the faint possibility of retaliation – reminds Kumar so much of his father that for the rest of the day, barring that quarter of an hour when he briefs her on her first writing project in years that she might or might not have desired, he can only slouch over his desk, twiddling with his pen, and jump into those memories of his father that never arrive alone, but in droves that stick to every inch of his surface until he can barely recognize himself.

He knows his father is not a good husband and, by extension, a good father, when three days before he is to be picked up from school for summer vacations, he is instead stuffed into Chief's white Ambassador that he only used for personal errands. They climb from the mountains where the school is situated, into the Himalayas farther north. The twists and turns of the climb unsettle his empty stomach, and he retches out of the car window, each bout worsened by the billows of exhaust smoke. For the next few days, he stays at a mansion nestled in the hills and accessed by a back road blocked to the rest of the town. Strudlhof steps lead into an enclosure of glass, the living room flanked by shadows of a large palash tree. It is a rather odd house, steps leading to landings leading to rooms and so on. Much of the house is made of glass, corners of some areas visible from others, which is especially the case with a grand library, where Kumar is often abandoned after breakfast with his father.

It is surprising, then, that Kumar never sees the woman of Chief's interest any of the sixteen times that he is a guest, served and taken care of only by the three brown servants in the colonial home of the lady. Except for a few minutes in the morning, Kumar never sees his father on those days, and on the last day, as they drive by the town again, Chief stops at a sports shop close to a college and buys him a willow bat. At school, Kumar leads a football team.

Kumar is only eight years old the first time around, and fifteen when he finally walks away from school a day before he suspects his father is due to arrive. He instead walks to a town nearby, where Aarav buys him a labelled bottle of whisky and a red-and-white packet of cigarettes.

✿

It, however, requires much more than lies and incentives to sever that love between child and parent that bolsters over years, over days and hours spent in adoration of each other. Though Kumar has seen less of Chief, and even less of his mother, who passed on as soon as he came of age, he still desires time with him – the kind that would belong to only themselves, paving the way for the bond they would share as two men in adulthood.

But after he is shipped off to boarding school – a trend started after the horrors that Bablu Nath had unleashed on those scarred cousins and sisters – Chief's presence becomes almost mythical. Besides those few hours spent in the Ambassador, and even fewer in the glass mansion, and an evening each in summer and winter vacations at the ancestral home in Ahmedabad, he fails to see his father at all. Those few exceptions never allow Kumar to enquire after his father's work, or if there would ever be a possibility of the two being like Aarav and his father, and the time never arises. By the age at which children set sail from their shores for years, Kumar learns that he will remain fatherless even if Chief fits the figurehead; he had already been disinterested for several years.

Kumar only comes to truly despise his father the evening he hears the story of how he – his father, Chief – came to be known as such, a moniker he kept as close to his heart as one might keep their sole prized jewel or a family heirloom, for the sixteenth time. The Mehtas are gathered at their ancestral residence for Diwali, more at the insistence of Kumar's grandparents – now senile and barely understandable, as people of a certain age in anxious throes of battle with their now inexplicable mortality tend to be – than any kinly affection. Kumar's aunts, Chief's sisters, hover in tentative circles around them, conversing with his docile mother about those homebound matters that largely make sense only to women.

If only reluctantly, they care for the small woman who sometimes cakes her skin with foundation and powder where Chief's hands leave angry welts. Poorly – perhaps intentionally so. These gatherings are the few times when Kumar sees his mother speak and laugh – as much as a few giggles could be called so. Here, he learns that she once obsessively collected Banarasi silk saris and kept long accounts of movies she watched. One of Chief's youngest sisters pushes Kumar's mother to retell the story of when she followed Raj Kapoor to Mumbai.

Kumar does not know this woman. A woman who seeks adventures and information, who obsesses and fixates. He only knows his mother – unspeaking and absent. A doll of pale porcelain staring out of her bedroom window.

They ask Kumar about his studies or his captaincy of the football team – it was rather astounding that they, who lived several latitudes and longitudes away, knew more about him than his father, who has at least some inkling of involvement in his existence. But their brother, they avoid completely, and not just in the way families mired in property disputes usually do, or like siblings – now old and too familiar with each other's terrible habits – tend to, but as if Chief were a dark abyss, threatening to pull them into disaster.

Kumar remains, and will remain, unaware of those secrets the generations before him have carried to their graves. But he grows up resentful. While his schoolmates often miss days to attend weddings of cousins, or when they become men, travel the world with them, he stays alone, his only social bind being Aarav, who avoids his family ties of his own accord. Adulthood stokes that resentment, devoid of all familial duties, until one day he decides he needs no one – a conviction so strong, he holds onto it dearly till the day he dies.

✿

It is a story he has heard many times before. Bablu Nath Mehta invited, in the last week of his time in New York City, to one of the world's leading literary magazines. Bablu Nath, in these years, has become a young man, experienced all those harangues and liberties that shed the last of the doubts of a boy, propelling him into a conceited manhood. His friend John's brother is a writer at the magazine, and after much convincing, arranges a meeting between them – or as Bablu Nath thinks, a conference between great minds. Now we must remember that those early days of a name twisted and marred till they brought tears to Bablu Nath as a toddler, have receded from his mind. Neither the list of appellations nor the faces of those friends, who are now men in small managerial positions, remain of importance to him. But memories work in mystical ways, the mind and body forgetting the event itself but remembering inconsequential details – a child fallen into a sewer might remember the colour of the shoelaces he wore that day or a sick bird he had been chasing, but can barely recall, at times not at all, the actual time spent in wait for his mother to notice his absence or for a passerby to hear his meek pleas for help. Of more consequential memories are those lingering feelings of fear, doom and panic – those definitive emotions that trump even long-past sensations of joy and excitement.

To his friends in the new city, he no longer goes by Bablu Nath anymore; he goes by 'Babs' – what John calls him the first time they meet. In his friends' words, he never suspects any ill intentions, and though not the most ideal of nicknames, he abandons the need to maintain a strong sense of identity in favour of being in the good books of those he considers superior to his brothers in the motherland. All of it changes the day he sets foot into the sprawling headquarters of the magazine and witnesses the centre of literary discourse, one that he has only absorbed and admired from afar – the only way most people do when they hold books or periodicals in their hands – through his own eyes. The cacophony of dozens of typewriters labouring in tune with each other, the sting of cigarette smoke leaving a suspended smog near the ceiling, the sound of secretaries' heels, of phones answered and the clacking of rotary dials finally germinate that seed of his hopes and dreams that had kept him from graduating from law school.

Bablu Nath meets the writer. John takes him to his table – no office, just desks and desks placed haphazardly throughout the large hall that serves as the headquarters; the same arrangement that he would later emulate in the offices of *The Narrator* – and introduces him to his brother. He is tall and blonde, the very definition of beauty to Bablu Nath, and when he talks of Evelyn Waugh and Richard Wright, the glint of wonder that shines in the writer's eye is similar to the one that stokes Bablu's thoughts before he puts himself to sleep. The two talk at length, mostly of the lack of defining works from the East – Keith, the brother, thinks it's the certain lack of literary acumen, perhaps worsened by the British Raj, though according to Bablu Nath, it's a collective laziness that plagues the country on the brink of Independence. They discuss their favourite writers – 'Fitzgerald leaves the reader nostalgic for the golden era that he has never seen' – and the more nuanced, 'I have no sympathies for any other state than capitalism. If anyone has their doubts, they should read Rand's work.'

Bablu Nath leaves reluctantly, pausing with every movement – when he grabs his hat and coat, when he stubs out his cigarette, when he shakes the men's hands goodbye – like a lover sadly looking over his shoulder for a word of reason from the woman to stay just a bit longer. When he finally turns around, the writer says, 'See you around, Chief'.

It is, however, never as simple as 'See you around, Chief' during these gatherings. It twists and squeezes, breaks and fixes, stretches and coils, like stories do when they are passed on from one person to another, or in this case from Bablu Nath to Chief and the various editions of him over time. Sometimes, it is Chief's great ambition, so unlike the specimen of other Indians that the writer has seen, and other times, it is his inexhaustible knowledge of literature and the written word that compels the writer – 'my friend, Keith' – to call him so.

But in that moment, as he watches his father regale his family with this anecdote that they have heard so many times that it is as much a fixture of their Diwali gathering as Lakshmi *puja*, Kumar cannot help but wonder if his family knows something about his father, the way he knows of the many affairs he maintains or the many silences he buys from the women he batters in these affairs.

Eventually, the father too comes to loathe his son as he fails to be the image of everything he failed to achieve himself, and instead becomes a reflection of all that he despises in himself. Kumar is too rebellious, too inciting – he rages, is pig-headed, often self-destructive. Angry and arrogant, so unlikely to listen to adults that for the last year his mother is alive, she refuses to see his face. Reports from school call him a menace, detailing cases of lower-class men locked in cobwebbed sheds and beaten on the field. Money for a new wing in the library, donated by his grandfather, keeps him in the matches.

Instead of an English or American school, he chooses a local university. Instead of a serious vocation, he studies literature. Kumar mocks his father when he is berated for his choice of university education, only to be reminded of Chief's time with the writer, which would not have occurred – consequently every event that transpired since that serendipitous meeting, including Kumar himself and *The Narrator* – if it wasn't for law that he had intended to study. Chief believes it is Aarav, the debonair young friend who had more opinions on literature and cinema than a critic. The boy, fed and dressed by a family of protestors and activists, would not let their eldest son go abroad for an education that he could receive in his homeland. It is surprising that Chief, usually perceptive enough to know whom to manipulate and who could potentially manipulate him – in modern words, a steady narcissist – was unable to see the reflection. He had only met Aarav a few times, enough to fill him with a deep distrust for the boy who spoke as if his word was last, and seemed to hear the words of others only to shred them apart with ancient rhetoric and bullying logic.

Now, Kumar has turned away from the truth of Aarav's actions, much like he had done all those years ago with his father. Instead of holding his mother's gaze, he preferred – found it easier to – simply consider her gone before her time had arrived. To let days remain the same was simpler, like it was simpler to pretend that it was some other Aarav with some other father influenced by alcohol, Western modernities, nagging women; an Aarav he did not know, who had perhaps grown up away from those dorm rooms and in the shadow of some other friends; who was not even a national gem or a revered artist – who had raped several women.

As her back recedes through the doors of his office and her clunky figure walks to her desk, where she, like a machine, picks up the topmost paper and begins slashing and correcting like a schoolteacher, he is once again filled with resentment towards his dead father. Towards Aarav – the son Chief would have deserved if sons truly grew into images of their father.

SEVEN

One often discovers the purpose behind an action much later. It is not introspection or retrospection. There is no active analysis of a past decision made in a moment of strange impulsivity. Like those discoveries made beside fireplaces or questions of great scientific importance solving themselves amid a game of tennis, those past actions – simply dormant and gathering life – one day come to reveal their reasons.

In the weeks following Kumar's instructions – 'Give me an impressive piece on the city's frescoes. One week in the city. Accommodations and meals paid for. A guide will pick you up at the railway station and accompany you' – she finds herself driven by wayward and rather abnormal impulses. The memories of Aarav, replete with the smell of stale smoke that had replaced the scent of cologne in that forced nearness, mark the beginning of her day and the end of her night. In the interim, she dreams of scenarios concocted by a desperate mind. Was there a need to agree to look at his new script? Was there a need to be present on the occasion? Was there a need to continue working with Kumar of the brutal friend?

Her grandfather, though as stoic as any man who toiled until his palms were like leather, had enjoyed only one indulgence in his long life – bootleg cassettes of *Hasya Kavi Sammelan*. The two – eldest and youngest – would sit together on the sofa, the younger imitating the poised engrossment of the other: legs crossed, one hand on the armrest, the other supporting the chin. She, however, found it difficult, if not completely impossible, to maintain that posture, for the cassettes came through with the funniest jokes – about drunks falling into sewers, about men chased by donkeys, and the classic: a wife running after her husband with a rolling pin. At the last one, her grandfather's lips would stretch into a smile, and, unable to imagine her mother threatening her father but aching to impress and bond with her grandfather, she too would laugh.

One day, the cassette screeched – '*Char Lainaa Suna Raha Hoon, Char Lainaa Suna Raha Hoon, Char Lainaa, Char Lainaa ...*' Her grandfather had waited several long minutes, that proclamation of four lines running hundreds of times in that duration, until even that declaration dissipated into the mingled sounds from the B-side.

These impulses now come like those four words declaring those four lines, repeatedly hurtling through her mind until she acts on them. It never satisfies whichever itch compels her to move – her legs, her fingers, her eyes in the direction that would fulfil the most immediate impulse. But in the moment right after, and for a few seconds until another impulse begins its screeching repetition, her mind quietens; it takes on the same calmness and relative serenity as those of more stable psyches.

It begins in the office itself, a few days after Kumar hands her a document. It is a list, several points to be remembered on the work trip to the city of frescoes: always stay with Mahendra, your guide; go wherever he suggests in the itinerary, listen to the owners of these *havelis*; note down the shapes and colours of the frescoes, ask after their histories. She is to be a journalist, a profession she has never been before, not even in the times of Chief, when her writings were of the vaguer and more philosophical acumen, as those of youthfully novel introspection tend to be. Now she is to prod and enquire, listen and ask, take tea with several men and women, perhaps even attend some evening arranged in her name.

The anticipation of this duty, so long overdue in its arrival and so painful in its existence in her hands, gnaws at her like splinters buried too deep into the skin and difficult to pull out. From her desk, she watches Jagannath, once again swaying on his feet, rather lazy after his lunch break, during which he was known to tipple often. Poonam arranging a slip of ideas for the next edition in the sequence she ascertains to be the most to least fit for Kumar's eyes. Mahesh struggling over an article that might not make its way to her desk this time to be corrected until it was less blue of his pen and more red of her furious suggestions. The shapes of their bodies and the small fidgeting of their beings are loud, like drums beating in the dead of night. Inexplicably, she is vexed by the tapping of Poonam's heels on the footrest of her chair and the loud crunching sounds coming from the desk behind her, where one of *The Narrator*'s oldest employees, Rajesh, sits.

She takes her head in her hands, leaning onto her desk, which wobbles a few times under the weight before settling on one side. Until it does, she clenches her teeth. *I could smash this table into the wall,* she thinks. Instead, another impulse rises from the onslaught.

Right in her line of sight is her pencil. Her stomach growls, and she wonders if she can eat graphite. She keeps it at bay for several seconds, distracting herself with some specimens of similar articles Kumar has left for her. But the pencil speaks to her, its dirty brown resembling some of the food that the cook at Mrs Pradhan's makes. Her eyes flit between the article and the pencil. When they tire, she lifts the pencil and takes a bite of its sharpened end. It breaks easily, wood and graphite weakened with wilting. When she chews, a splinter almost goes through her gums, and afraid of the added costs she might accrue, she spits it onto her table – a garbled mess of wood and blackened saliva. From across the room, Poonam watches her with disgust.

✿

This impulse, however, does not become a problem until one day – one of the last in the week before she leaves for the city of frescoes – resting against a pillar in the courtyard and listening to Mrs Pradhan regale her with a story of her youthful adventures, she feels the calls of a compulsion. Till now, they have been relatively harmless. This very impulse too is innocuous. She is not tempted to rage or throw stones and books at people. Women's fury rarely compares to men's, their uniqueness and infrequency making them poetic wonders, romanticized and infantilized. Some would argue that women have more reasons to rage, their patience eroded by the hot blood of others. But it is only in our imaginations, where justices denied in reality find their rightful place with the logical and reasonable; here, those who scream the loudest are the best heard.

Her impulses remain odd, even rather amusing. She eats a bug here, punches a hole in Kumar's car there. She runs after a rabid dog she has seen several times in her street and steals an onion from a costermonger when he is not looking. Until now, it is not harmful – or rather, not harmful to others. Her stomach aches from the bug; her knuckles remain unmoving for several days after she unleashes her anger at the metal of Kumar's car. The rabid dog turns back at her, drawing the attention of several others until she is running so fast her heart threatens to give up. Only the stolen onion remains fruitless, thrown into the basket that Mrs Pradhan keeps for potatoes and onions.

Mrs Pradhan's nutcracker catches her eye long before the beginnings of these impulses. She loves the pattern of vines and bunched fruits on its handles. *It must be uncomfortable to wield,* she thinks, but never asks Mrs Pradhan about it. The nutcracker itself belongs in a silver-gilded box, lined with purple velvet and severely slotted for various assortments that go into sustaining the ancient addiction of opium. Every evening, from a hidden spot that she never learns of, Mrs Pradhan brings it out into the gallery. The woman is meticulous with it, most of the rheumatic clumsiness abandoned for the pleasures and numbness of aches that would follow.

In her first year with Mrs Pradhan, in moments of desperation, she plans an escape from her past with the help of the nutcracker. She could carry away the entire box, along with those small brown, almost black pellets, the absence of which leaves Mrs Pradhan jittery – like that one time she had to be sent to a government-permitted *bhang* shop, where other addictives are sold to regulars. Now, she just wants to deprive someone of their small sustenance, as she had been innumerable times before – to snatch away the most beloved, like her will to live – the most beloved, as it should be in most, had once been snatched from her.

In that moment, however, she does not know what propels her to eye the nutcracker with such longing and such intent. On her way to the railway station, she finds Mrs Pradhan open-mouthed and shallowly breathing in her stupor. She never meets Mrs Pradhan again, even though while swiping the nutcracker, she decides that when she returns from the city of frescoes, she will find a way to rebuild the association of dependency the two share. She will think of an excuse in the interim, give it as much time as she is giving to the article on the city of frescoes. She will bring Mrs Pradhan to trust her again. We rarely know when we say our final goodbyes to people, and Mrs Pradhan, though vexed, but mainly saddened, forgives the tenant whom she knows to be the culprit. She does expect her to return soon and hopes she would bring with her the nutcracker, but when years pass and no news of her former tenant is ever heard, she considers the nutcracker lost much like the young woman, and perhaps even with the young woman.

✿

It is not the city but the work that she finds dull from the moment she steps into the city of frescoes. It has been rather long since she travelled between places farther away, ones that required rubbing shoulders with hurrying people, sitting long hours in uncomfortable seats and enduring the presence of intrusive strangers. She is relieved when she alights from the train, enough that the forceful, almost harassing solicitations of the porters blocking her way to the platform feels welcome, palatable after the horrors of being advised on her marriage-less state by all those she had shared the berth with.

Near the entrance, as crowded as the inside with waiting passengers or those waiting for passengers, she finds Mahendra. She spots him in the distance right away, holding up a placard bearing Kumar's name rather than hers, as if she too belonged to him; as if her identity was yet not of enough importance to be recognized by others. She feels a little jilted when he doesn't catch her with the same promptness – his eyes rove over her approaching figure several times. Around her, women with covered heads and children picking their noses, little girls adjusting their pigtails bump and jostle into her, and though surprised, she finds it offensive that in the eyes of an observer, she is no different from them. Her education, her work, her social standing – which she is conditioned to consider higher than several and lower than several more – do not make her any different from millions of others.

Till she struggles through the thick of the crowd, and until she reaches Mahendra, her guide in the city of frescoes, she harbours a humming resentment against him. It isn't simply that Kumar did not provide her name, it is that Mahendra never tried to learn more about the person he would be escorting, once again leaving her to bear the weight of her dubious identity. But it is short-lived, rather feeble. Mahendra, from the first words he speaks, is buoyant. Chipper.

'What's in a name?' he quotes when she enquires about the absence of her name on the placard and, quickly grabbing her bags, walks her to an Ambassador. It is the first time she has met someone of such jocosity; mischief dances in his beady eyes and his lips quiver perpetually, stifling words he prefers not to say in the company of the 'fairer sex' – in English, as he puts it. In the car, which he drives with abandon, with the kind of nonchalance that comes not from a disregard for life, but rather from faith in divine protection, he beguiles her with stories of the places they will go. In Mahendra's excitement – the words he uses, the large gestures of his hands that leave the steering wheel often, and the questions about her interests – she too fidgets in her chair with eagerness, the first signs of a smile appearing at the corner of her lips.

'It isn't really a trip to the fort if you don't threaten to throw kids into the crocodile-infested moat,' he says.

'Whose kids?' she asks, taken in by his pause, accented by the jovial raise of his eyebrows.

'Any kids. There are plenty at the fort.'

Throughout the long drive to his house, Mahendra never stops talking, his laugh sometimes rumbling louder than the sound of the whirring engine. It is odd when he asks her questions, then more questions based on her responses. They aren't the burning queries of elders meant to provide a bearing for the standing of their own children or as a sounding board for boasting about their better luck. Mahendra has that one quality that she has never found in anyone she has met. He is a listener for the sake of it. For the sake of knowing. He is as curious as that inquisitive child from a distant past. In the moments he waits for her to answer his questions, she thinks, *This is what a person becomes if he retains the wonderment of his childhood.*

'I grew up not so far from here, but never came to the city. There were some havelis around the town, and I saw some frescoes,' she responds – more words than she has spoken to anyone else before. 'But never as beautiful as the ones here.'

The hour-long journey from the railway station to Mahendra's house is not enough. As soon as he parks near the entrance of a newly built house – perhaps a recent investment on family land – she begins to miss the ease she feels in his presence. In the central courtyard, towered over by two storeys of rooms, he leaves her bags to introduce her to his parents. The women come out of a traditional kitchen – dingy and sooty. They wipe their hands on their saris before greeting her. It is a peculiar greeting, one of maternal warmth so unfamiliar that for the next hour she spends eating with and talking to them about her work at *The Narrator,* she fights back tears of nostalgia for the times that were not, but could have been.

✿

Mahendra, however, is still her guide, still in the employ of her employer. He carries with him an itinerary, a handwritten copy of which he leaves on a chair beside her door the next morning. For the first few minutes after breakfast, in the Ambassador it is just her and Mahendra. She puts a relaxed elbow on the window and lets Mahendra guide the tone of the day – loquacious, mischievous.

He describes to her in detail the paunches and hairy ears of some of the haveli owners. Mahendra is, she learns, particularly amused by the unshapeliness of the rich and the well-fed, and though rather inappropriate, he paints such a vivid picture that she begins to note down his words. Mahendra and his family themselves are as lithe as one would expect toiling farmers to be, and in her own slight wobbliness – even the same shapelessness that Mahendra mocks – she feels slightly unclothed. But it is not a mockery of bodies. It is Mahendra's way of dealing with the injustice he knows exists, the one that keeps his mother and father working to the bone, and him, a man of multitudinous languages, from becoming anything more than a guide. In fact, it is this very mastery of eleven languages that most dazzles her. It is Raju of Dev Anand come alive.

An older couple joins them in the car on their way to a haveli, some minutes later. She feels hurt as if in the short time, less than a day that she and Mahendra have spent together, she has developed a friendship with him that does not need the intrusion of others. She pulls her hand away from the window and straightens herself, her back resting flush against the chair.

The couple – American – turn their noses up at Mahendra's accent, often asking him to repeat words that must have been clear the first time. A few times, they titter to themselves, whispering in that conspicuous way that is always meant to be heard. It is laughable, their disdain, when they themselves can barely wrap their tongues around even one language.

✿

At the havelis, Mahendra recedes, letting the owners or the family members present there guide the tourists. The frescoes, some of the most beautiful creations she has ever seen, leave her so overwhelmed that the pit of her stomach thrums with giddiness. When the owners see the gleam in her eyes, they ask her to touch the frescoes – some painted laboriously over marble and some simply in hidden corners, on stone and cement, now fading. Of the owner, the foreigners get the words without trouble and when she turns around to catch sight of Mahendra, to share with him a look of intimacy as if to say, *are you seeing this?*, she sees only his back framed by doors or windows, lazily smoking a cigarette.

Though bored, she still takes notes of the oleanders and grapevines, vases of camellias and chrysanthemums, portraits and profiles of lowly warriors and generals, of frivolous noblewomen framed in motifs of Mughal influence. Sometimes, in tapestries, an artist leaves behind a work of his imagination – a couple possibly embracing under a parasol, a woman's breast left uncovered from her *choli*, an elephant with seven legs instead of four. In the palaces and forts, the frescoes become grander, spanning walls and enchanting ceilings with hallucinatory whorls and flora. Under the cover of such richness, she forgets for brief moments the hurts and betrayals, past and present.

When she retires for the night, after several servings that Mahendra's mother and his equally genial father insist upon, she sleeps without faces tormenting her in her dreams – until one night, it is just the stolen nutcracker that worries her.

Except for those few moments in Mahendra's car, the two are never alone even though she desires nothing more than to bask in his easy company. Mahendra is nothing more than a good-natured stranger, but with his affable presence, he appears to be an old friend – one she might have known for decades, with whom she might have once played with in the mud, or forced to play the reticent husband in childhood games.

Often, when it is just the two of them – on their way to pick up tourists who are his ardent clients, or en route to a new haveli, having exhausted places of busier footfalls – she implores Mahendra to accompany her to long-forgotten ruins on the outskirts of the city. A haunted fort, not yet famous, becomes paramount. She insists and urges, begs and pleads, but Mahendra never relents.

'Kumar sir would have me out of this job,' he says, his friendliness slipping in those moments.

She never pushes further – until the next car ride, soon after they leave the other tourists at their hotels.

It is in the nature of associations to end. The dearest friendships fizzle and fade, large distances lead to outcomes one never anticipates, and the faces of those we once loved blur around the edges, the colour of their eyes and the shapes of their noses and mouths erasing until formless. Of all she has loved transiently, Mahendra is perhaps the briefest.

At the telegraph office, tidings, whether good or bad, await her.

Tauji passed away.

First words she hears from her mother in five years.

PART 2

THE VALLEY

EIGHT

In a different era, the woman of the forest, briefly forgotten, now turns her face towards the heat of the spring sun rays. Radha runs a hand over the smooth, stretched skin of her stomach, caressing and cooing to the child within. She traces the path of her husband's gentle and searching fingers from the night before. In her time away, he has aged as if days had been years. His cheeks droop with a haunting anguish, which she suspects to be her doing, but does not wish to confirm. The first night, he embraces her in fury – his calloused fingers dig into her paltry flesh and she responds with the greed and ardour of earthly possession.

When the snow clears and the thick roofs of huts sprout wild grass, his enmity dies. He is not a man given to grudges or anger, rather of the clement mien that is often perceived to be naivete or even dullness. His forgiveness does not come in waves; one day, he simply forgets her imprudence. Forgives it. Now his fingers trace the girth of her growing middle with love. Wonder. Devotion. When he pulls her closer, it is with tenderness, as if carrying the fragile frame of his child. In such moments, he appears like the boy of their frivolous youth again – his face drawing back into the firmness of his years, stretched and taut with a gleeful smile, and the bereavement that floats within his eyes receding into the depths of his soul.

With the return of the hotter months, the timber company sets up its outpost farther. Closer to the village, the forest is denuded of teak and sal. The English sahib responsible for the outpost remains at his bungalow on the outskirts of the village. But he and others are instructed to raise a flimsy, thatched structure anyway.

'For the sahib, if he wishes to rest during the day,' says a crony.

He – the husband – leaves earlier than before, those years entwined in the warmth of one another now experienced for shorter hours. The demand for wood never eases, and with the war unfolding in a distant land, the fellers swing and strip and sweat longer and harder. He untangles himself from the snaring limbs of Radha with chagrin. On the long walk through their forest of chir, at the outpost where he waits for his instructions, walking behind Draupadi – the gentle behemoth who carries the logs he fells – while his arms ache from the impact of blade on bark, his mind remains with Radha.

Radha too awakens perplexed, the warmth long withdrawn. Under their thick blanket, she searches for the figure of her man, but the depression on the mattress is cold, his scent of wood and cones almost indistinct from the mouldy one of the fabrics. It is her child that wakes her with impatient kicks and turns, cocooned within the quilt of her womb. Much like her, he too is of the forest. He craves the dance of the wind in his mother's hair, the tickling badgering of falling leaves on her stomach. He erupts with joy at the inquisitive cawing of crows, and turns and tumbles with the frantic games of squirrels.

Radha drags their charpoy to the courtyard, where she remains until the sun sets behind the snowy mountain, and she senses him draw his axe one last time for the day on the weeping woods of her forest.

✿

In the daytime, Radha remains close to the squeezed quarters of the village's huts. From the charpoy, she watches women crouch close to their smouldering *kangri*, the smell of cooking quail in one courtyard melding into the simmering beets in another. Before, they would stand at their thresholds and bellow towards her house. The sickening insincerity of the world beyond has not yet crawled into their hearths and Radha's intimacy with the forest is invaluable. The people here are no strangers to the miracles hiding under their feet and snaking against the walls of their homes. But Radha senses the heart of the forest as if it beats a loud melody to call her to itself.

A pheasant need not call its mate for Radha to know where it forages and hides. She walks towards the brambles and watches, and when she walks – straight-backed and determined – the pheasant lowers its tail and surrenders. A death at her hands does not feel like an end. A child born to her could be blessed and gifted like her – after all, pheasants, quails and hares often found their way into the villagers' homes, greasy with ghee and fragrant with the herbs Radha picked on her way back. In the hopes of quickening her womb, they brought stews and teas; steaming rice when Radha spent the day collecting firewood, when her thrumming nearness to the forest was still amusing, when she had not disappeared and returned as if a living ghost.

Now the women avert their eyes when they hear the scraping of Radha's charpoy being dragged out of her home, or when, supporting the weight of her growing middle, she lowers herself onto it with discomfort. From over the smoke of the kangri, they peruse her with fearful curiosity. The smile she had worn when leaving her home remains stretched across her face with mirth. Her demeanour benign and adoring.

It is envy, malice. It is the dedication of her husband. The fanatical strength of her will. The forest slaps their skin raw in the winters and stings and pricks in its asceticism, but gifts her barren womb with a child. It isn't so much the peculiar joy on her face and the affection that drips from her gaze – it is their own suspected iniquity that turns them away from her.

Radha herself is oblivious to the sneering noses turned up at her, or to the whispered, loathsome expressions that accompany her mentions. Her remedies and monastic administrations to the sick are eschewed. Vital but forsaken. Husbands hack and hawk, mothers wail with unseen aches, feet fester with wounds from the earth – an easier fate to swallow than the eerie benevolence of the woman, or witch, resting across from their homes. Radha alone plucks the purple flowers of felsworts and remorsefully uproots the azure of gentian. When she finds a yew growing near their daphne bushes, she is reminded of her second mother. Her heart tugs briefly, and she searches faster. Her child would never snivel nor cry from ills.

✿

It is the man who worries in her stead. Though Radha returns, she sheds the girlish manners that had earlier ensnared the village around her fingers. The harmless roundness of her youth is chiselled and sliced into imperceptible sharpness. Under the burbling waters of her calm lurks a mystical current. If he dips his hands too deep, they might return bloodied and lacking a few fingers. Her scent of jasmine and honeysuckle fades. Now, when he presses his nose into her thick hair, she smells like the earth after long rains. Simple and coarse. Like monkshood.

The men are not inclined to talk of their women or matters that bring to the surface their humanity or ordinariness. Behind Draupadi and others of the herd, they walk in sombre, tired silence. The way back home is long, and from the back comes raucous laughs and glib remarks. There is the stumbling walk of a drunk, and in the front, the hollow sound of a palm meeting his back. The women have long since murmured their fears and doubts into their men's ears. It is with some hesitation, but eventually they enquire. Words feigned with concern. Tinged with discomfort.

How did she return? Did you have to look for her more? Was she truly uninjured? Might she have wandered too far? Lost? Do you suspect any weakening of the mind?

Under their words, he hears the true questions.

Did she elope with an old lover?

Is it really your child?

My wife has seen her staring towards the thick of the forest for hours.

She talks to her child, as if reminding or informing him of what lies beyond.

As if waiting for someone's arrival.

Spring has returned when Radha feels her child's anticipation gnaw at the insides of her womb – eager and impatient. He drums a soft tune to the rising beats of her heart.

Near the company outpost, he caresses Draupadi's long snout. So far from home, he is not aware of the aches in which Radha loses herself. He is still thinking of Radha's skin and scent as he runs a bristled brush over Draupadi's tough hide. Radha's uncertain feet and hurried actions are lost within the grove of chir that lies between them. Even if he were near, it is not his duty; a task she must complete on her own. The forest that gives her the child beckons her to deliver him into its lap.

In the familiar shadows of her hut, she finds herself suddenly uncomfortable in the company of their worldly possessions. She kicks at a kangri; its coal tumbles out in a sooty trail. The blanket, she throws out the door. It is not enough to swathe her child in. He will wear pelts in the winter – kingly and magical. She leaves the charpoy outside to be harangued by the kindlier erosions of nature, but within the hut, she disturbs their few tumblers and the glinting set of plates and bowls of steel that he buys to mark their new beginnings. But the discomfort within her demands more – to match without the turmoil within. Every few minutes, her child announces his impending arrival louder, with larger declarations. His restlessness grows, gnawing lower towards the ground, until she is hurrying out of their home and back into the forest where the child will be born.

The ways of the forest are unknown. Its guiding hands and absolute directives unheard to the ears of those who refuse to believe. Their hut is not where her son will take his first breaths. It will not be the charpoy or under the matronly charge of the other women. He will not see the face of his father nor the composed attentiveness of the midwife. It will not be the clean colonnades of chir nor the secluded cover of deodars.

Her feet drag her deeper into the thick of the forest. The timber company has not spread itself into this side yet, and the forest is rich with uninterrupted undergrowth. Ferns tickle at her feet and catch in the threads of her sari. She stops beside a chilgoza and discards her clothes. A few steps from it is a cover under a young sprout of fragrant bay, where she lies supine, waiting for her child.

✿

When he returns from the outpost, the course of his day is decided by the people gathered around his hut. They brandish sticks, prodding at the blanket discarded near their charpoy as if the corpse of a wandered dead animal. No kangri burns in the courtyard, nor does Radha wait to welcome him into her arms. He throws his face into his calloused hands and cries. The first time, he loses his mother. Almost loses Radha. Now what could be taken from him if not her? Their child? This second time, his faculties leave him.

But much like the memories of the first time that he has shovelled into painful corners, she arrives once again. In her frail arms, she carries a fleshy bundle. Their son, covered in slime and blood. The villagers do not see her right away, and it is still some time before they notice the lack of cover on her. The men avert their gazes, but the women, though briefly shocked, run towards her with the discarded blanket. He distantly hears them fussing on their way to her, screaming at her not to strain herself and admonishing her for the state she has put herself in. Their indifference towards her is momentarily disregarded.

Radha, however, shuffles towards him, her gaze fixed on his. She ignores the women who run towards her, the blanket stretched between them, ready to be enfolded around her bare body. She waves them away with a shake of her head. There is no shame in her state – her son is born in his skin, and she too is reborn, as she had been the first time. When he raises his head completely, she smiles triumphantly at him. *Did I not say that we will have a son?* He remains crouching, too afraid to approach this creature of the forest. She is not a woman, nor a beast. Radha is a divination among men.

✿

For the first few days, he frets until Radha gently instructs him to leave for the outpost once again. He hovers over her shoulders, every fumble now making him mumble God's name. 'The child screamed and cried when he dropped to the earth,' she informs him, 'and he has no reason to do so anymore.' They remain in the courtyard for most of the day, on the dirty ground, the charpoy untouched in a corner, and the blanket that had failed to cover Radha's skin now abandoned at the edge of the village where the women had dropped it. Each morning, with the parting hoots of owls departing for their homes and those of sparrows and sunbirds chirruping their wakefulness, she brings the child outside and places him on the ground.

Though Radha's words soothe his paternal mind, away from their home, a different form of disquiet claws at him. The child stares, unfocused, at the many inches of his face – first his eyes, then ears, his nose, the smattering of sun spots around his temples and cheeks, at the full lips that are now also his own and the stubbly growth of an unkempt beard. He feeds when it is time, simply wiggling in his place to demand his mother's attention. He burps and sleeps like a child, and stares adoringly at Radha like a child.

But there is something peculiar about his son nonetheless. Under the sun, when the village women arrive in throngs, bearing food for Radha during the daytime, the oddities remain unperceived. He is an unusual child in his serenity and satisfaction with the world. At night, when the hours slow and he stares long and adoring into his son's eyes, the father sees a ring of yellow. Feline. Beastly. In the dying light of their kerosene lamp, he peers carefully into the eyes of his son. He suspects that it's the light of the lamp. Regardless, there is never enough reason to look any closer in the hours of the day when it could be inspected. In his dreams, he sees a beast of the forest – its thick paws crawling silently over the littered ground.

To Radha, it is no surprise, rather an inevitability that her son be of the forest. Like her mother had been. Her mother before her, and her mother before her. Like herself. He howls like a beast, bellowing its arrival into the lap of nature. But it is not with some latent sadness for leaving the comforts of his mother, rather the promise of grandeur that lies ahead of him in the many decades to come. It is then necessary that he be raised with the forest within his grasp at all times.

The village women who had previously averted their eyes let their quibbles lie dormant for the time being. Children in the village are rare – they die in their infancy, more often in the womb. Those afflictions that only discomfort the adults take children like the plague. Sons who live until their second decade are an anomaly, and the village recognizes the urgency of such moments. With the birth of every child, many who had turned their faces away forever, come back together. Their village has only one midwife – the oldest woman, now that Radha's second mother is deceased. But she is not a skilled woman, not like the one in the forest of Bhanj, who was known to have eased the arrival of many children with simple concoctions. Children die in canals, cease breathing in the open air; they cry once at their new fate and stop the next second. So it is that Radha's son becomes a fixture in the women's routines, and the men wake earlier and fell more timber to gather resources. Winter is still some time away, but in the meantime, the rains will batter their feeble hearths and leave vulnerable lungs at the mercy of the gods.

The forest itself leaves no marks on her. She has never slipped on a mossy stone in the river where many others have crushed their skulls from a hard fall. No thorn has ever pricked her; neither beast nor prey has taken her for anything other than a silent companion. The child is as much hers as he is the forest's.

It is, however, the suspicion of a presence that prickles at the back of her neck. She notices it during childbirth, as if the cover of undergrowth reveals her to curious, cunning eyes – but in those moments, her purpose is singular, her world confined to the tickling leaves of the bay and the sensation of her child sliding from her. The presence now comes with the wind when she is turned away from the edge of the village, and the downy hair on her body raises itself in fear. Sometimes, a shadow falls across her child's face, like a rain-heavy cloud separated from others. But when she looks over her shoulders, there is nothing but the large expanse of the clearing of their village – the shadow nothing but the swaying, prickly branches of the chir lining their home, disturbed by the mountainous breeze.

The child himself is unwary of what lurks in the shadows of the woods. It is his mother who is now leaving indelible marks in his early memories, and he absorbs the sun that bounces from her smooth skin when she leans over him to sing him songs. He does not notice the rosettes appearing and disappearing behind the long wild grass and trunks of ancient trees, nor the hungry eyes that track his uncertain, fragile movements.

✿

Secrets, however, stay hidden for only so long. It is the peak of day when Radha, having bathed and fed her child indoors, brings him out. She dusts the ground with the end of her sari, scurrying away ants and beetles that burrow into untouched spots of soil. They get into his ears at times, and he lies uncomfortable and fidgeting at night. The troubles die down by the morning, but she does not wish him to feel those few moments either.

It is the quiet that draws her attention. At this time of day, the sounds of the village seep into the flurry of the forest. Of women chattering excitedly into the coltish chatter of babblers and tailorbirds. Of the drumming labour of a woodpecker into the clanging of utensils and kangri. A call of a woman for her children to return for their midday meals is answered by the melodies of the orioles. But today, the forest stands still – the birds waiting with bated breath on their perch, leaves rustling only with the movement of the wind.

At the edge, where a grove blends soon into the understory of the virgin forest, she spots a shadow – robust and careful. It moves from behind a gigantic oak. Its muscles rippling and supple with every step of its noiseless paws. It steps into the path of a streak of light, and the darkened shadows that had covered its body now reveal a sprinkling of rosettes. Sensing the fearful eyes on itself, the leopard stalls and looks over with curiosity at the woman inspecting him.

It is uncommon for beasts of its bulk to wander this close to man's establishments. They are elusive. Recluses and hermits too privy to the dangers that lurk within man to walk beside them. The few times a starving or senile beast stalks in to carry away cattle, the Englishmen are quicker to arrive. They bring their rifles and lackeys and loud, clanging plates to drive the beast into range of their machines. The villagers sometimes tie an injured beast upside down to a tree to watch its slow and macabre demise over hours, but mostly, the Englishmen hoist their carcasses in their hands and take photographs of their game.

Radha is stunned. The unwonted apparition roots her to the earth. The child continues his cooing at her, unaware of her thundering blood. He is no longer a part of her flesh, and the distance leaves much to be understood. The beast's sudden disinterest jerks her back into the moment, and grabbing her unsuspecting son, she fences herself in the safety of her home.

✿

The decision is made less than a day later. Radha, who informs her husband about the beast, is not consulted on it. He borrows a claw trap from his white supervisors. The villagers watch fearfully when a man from the outpost helps him set it close to where Radha spotted the beast for the first time. 'It will clench around the paw of the leopard,' the man says, 'and the men can then beat him to death.' It is a brutal and despondent affair – one so unlike their character that the villagers recede into their homes with downturned, sombre eyes. He wishes he could have been lent the rifle, taught briefly its mechanics. It is an easier death, less gory. Radha places their son between their huddled bodies and sings to him – too occupied with worry for him to hear the strife that keeps her husband in a fitful sleep.

Close to the edge, they leave some grazing goats – bait for the leopard. The wait is long, days. The leopard is uninjured and healthy – its body still in its prime. It smells the herby scent of the goats' skin and the loud, salty one of the humans. Its primal needs drive it close to the village, though a sense of danger, an instinctive wariness, keeps it from moving forward. Perhaps its prudence eases the villagers' worry. Weeks after the sighting, they begin to spend less and less time in search of the beast. They stop turning their heads at rustling sounds from the bushes. A flurry of light at night, previously attributed to the glimmering eyes of a cat in the dark, simply becomes what it always is: fireflies alighting from their homes in search of another.

One day, the leopard stalks closer. Three of the goats that had been left at the edge have wandered far, two lost in the wilderness. The only one that remains is unwatched, grazing. It crouches lower in the thick of the ferns, its vision slightly marred by the overgrown leaves. The wind blows in the beast's direction, filling its head with the scent of the goat's fresh blood. It moves a careful limb forward, then another. A branch snaps under its hind leg, and the leopard pauses, waiting for the goat to hear of its impending end. The sound that follows with its next movement is unfamiliar, not one of nature. Dreadful. A metallic clang and click. The claw trap snaps around its paw, digging its iron teeth deep into flesh, tendon and muscle. The beast howls, drawing the attention of the villagers. The goat scurries away, and from where it disappears behind the huts, Radha's husband runs in with a baton in his hands. The others run behind him, shouting a war cry.

But the claw fails to close around the leopard's paw. The sound of metal clicking into place was too foreign. It is quick to draw back – even if man's machinations are often faster. It is still enough to pull its leg free from the device. When Radha's husband comes closer, the beast hisses and roars, writhes in its place. In pain. Afraid, he draws back – just enough to let the beast escape. In the trap, two claws of its right paw are all that remain.

It is Radha's innocence, her faith in her forest, that makes her bring the child into the courtyard the next day. No one sees the leopard when they trundle into the forest after it. In its wake, it leaves behind a trail of blood, harder to see as the forest thickens. 'It must have bled and died by now,' her husband says in the morning. 'No creature having thus been deprived of parts of itself, survives for long.'

Radha carries the child in her arms and inspects the forest beyond. The birds have taken up their usual chirrups. A coppersmith works away at a hollow tree somewhere close. Two treepies play in their bushes of daphne. She grabs the end of her sari and wipes away a spot on the ground, places her son down and kisses his glinting forehead. From within their hut, she fetches a basket of gentian flowers. She has collected their roots and distributed them to the villagers. The rains are difficult and leave them sniffling through the day. With the flowers, she will make a wreath of blue and place it over their cot.

But the wreath is not destined to be created. Radha will not witness the villagers struggle with cold through the monsoon, nor will she see her husband beat his chest in fury at his fate. Where she places her son, now remain only drops of blood – a small pool of it that trails into the forest. Her eyes remain on the trail as she walks, once again, into the belly of the verdant beast.

NINE

The rising din of the bus stop wakes her. She is sick from the long journey through winding hilly roads. Over every bump, the morning breakfast crawls higher towards her mouth, leaving between her teeth the taste of putrefied puri and sabzi and the burn of the syrupy chai that the driver had offered her in her seat. For the last leg, she rests her head on the dirty windowsill. Peanut shells and cigarette ends tickle her parched and peeling lips, but the slapping winds are comforting; their scent of evergreen foliage and simple provincial existence overpowers even the smoky exhaust that leaves a lingering path behind the creaking bus.

She has never been to the hills before – the coiling discomfort in her stomach is foreign, the dimming of sound terrifying, and the nausea that reaches her brain, painful. She has read books about these grand sentinels of her country, written in admiration of their sky-grazing peaks that are gentle and fertile – coquettish in their beckoning of a searching kindred soul, but formidable in their venerable grandiosity. These mountains are as intimidating as they are enticing, like a lover who seduces for the game of it. They fell armies and halt campaigns, seize the swords of conquerors. Men are humbled by the surfaces that strip away and shed the blinding, delicate façade to reveal sheer blocks of ice that even the bravest fear to summit.

The lower, rounded peaks, however, fall to the designs of man's ugliness. The bus stop is like every other she has seen. At the turn into the station, the driver honks aggressively at a woman shepherding her two children. The bus never slows, and the woman narrowly manages to pull her son out of death's moseying hands. When they stop, a new crowd pushes into her, driving her back into the bowels of the bus until she feels she would have to make the journey back to where she started. But the rabble settles like dust from a beaten carpet. Their journey is not to begin for another hour.

The city flanks a deafening river, its banks teetering with thousands of hotels and homes. She could have her pick from Hotel River View, Char Dham Hotel or Hotel Sunrise, but she moves towards a dharamsala where she can rest with the few monies to her name. Her arrival coincides with the celebration of *ekadashi*. Children painted in blue and sporting plastic snakes around their necks trudge through the crowd, hurling abuses at the slow trotters. She falls in the path of an older boy, and he curses her mother. Hordes slip and slide over the treacherous steps to the dirty waters of the river. When they emerge from their submersions, their hair glints with the filth from the sins of a hundred million devotees.

A woman leading her adolescent daughter reminds her of Mrs Pradhan; she is as fair as milk and her limbs balloon painfully at the joints. She feels the hard shape of the nutcracker through her backpack, but when the woman kicks a begging leper in his disfigured face, her guilt vanishes like his blessings of good marriage and healthy children for the young daughters.

Her presence in this holy city is one by chance – buses leading to trains that whistle through chaffed pastures and yellow fields. With the advertisement department at *The Narrator*, she often trimmed and embellished guarantees of peace and serenity. Shadowed images of yogis and godmen peering intensely at the turmoil within the hands that held them. With the weight of the nutcracker comforting her looming fear of sustenance and its make and heft anxiously scraping at her sensibilities, those claims of idyllic woods are what she recalls on the first train out of the city of frescoes.

She passes temples and shelters where dogs yip at her feet and unwashed sadhus shake their clattering *damrus* at her. At the red effigies under trees, likenesses of gods painted on walls and sacred trees tethered with thousands of strings, she tries not to feel disheartened. The promises of Himalayan tranquillity seem lost in appearances that she has seen innumerable times before – in the city of her tainted childhood, in darkened corners of her street and around the congested neighbourhood of *The Narrator*.

Her destiny, however, is a little farther ahead. At a travel agency, a man whisks her away from the roaring crowd. When she sees the guide at its doors, his eyes distantly watching the preparations for the evening prayers, it is as if he waits only for her and her deliverance at the doors of harmony.

Of her scant belongings from before, there remains even less now. She has left some of herself behind throughout her journey from the city of frescoes. The diary summing up her observations about the colourful frescoes in homes lies on a cushioned berth in a narrow-gauge train. An edition of a foreign magazine, given to her by Kumar to serve as guidance for her writing, fans its pages under dusty winds against the back of a station bench. Mahadevi Verma's face in a book stares up at a peeling ceiling in its abandoned exile in the room Mahendra had provided for her.

The guide, however, still insists on a porter. There is only one bag that she carries on her shoulders, but the porter is lean and hunched, the burden of the worldly attachments of others weighing his shoulders down towards his early grave. The porter smiles a rotten-toothed smile when she grudgingly hands him her bag, and the stink of fermenting bananas rises up her nose. By the time she begins walking again, he has already disappeared at a turn.

The dharamsala, she learns, is nestled in the mountains. A small valley that gets buried under snow in the winters leads to the abode of gods higher in the shoulders of the Himalayas. The gravel path twists and rolls under her feet, but the soft gurgling of the gentle river lazily running down beside her steadies her steps. When thick bushes of desmodium and wild bamboo shield the waters from her, she turns to the light music of woodpeckers beyond the thickets to her left and the tittering, playful chirrups of warblers and sunbirds.

She sniffs at blossoms of bergenia and balsam when sauntering mules pass her by, their earthy scent of dung and fur settling into her hair and woollen clothes. Farther up, when the noise of civilization gives way to the pleasant clatter of nature, she startles at the scurrying pikas that hide in the hollowed fallen logs and inspect her intrusion with twitching whiskers and pondering hands.

Her new guide, unlike Mahendra, is disinclined to talk. She fixes her eyes on his sure, sandal-clad feet when the paths become treacherous for her inexperienced ones. He leaves behind a trail of plastic wrappers of *jarda*; the emptied packets flutter in the soft breeze, marking their presence for others who seek some unrushed weeks.

At the foot of this mountain, surrounded by the smells and noise of millions, she could not overlook the chatter within herself either. The more she heard, the more her mind fidgeted, confused and overwhelmed. Beside the river, when she breathes, she recoils at the unrepenting cycles of existence – many months of transgression forgiven and forgotten in the flowing bosom of a goddess.

The misplaced culpability of others is, however, soon displaced by the peaks that lie before her. The mountains seem small and near, their cover of foliage indistinct in their appearance as verdant carpets. At a clearing, before they trek higher, she stands by a calm stream of her companion river and breathes in and out.

✿

A row of swishing tails welcomes her to the gates of the dharamsala. The docile mules flick their ears towards the sound of steps within the spacious grove of chir. From the thick, she can only see parts of them – a glimpse of a curious, gentle eye, the colourful knitting of an embellished saddle, uncertain hooves that beat at the ground with primal frustration. When she is closer, the pack pays her no mind. Her muted presence is one of safety – as much as can be with humans – and her short companion is familiar with the mules that often carry him back to where he will once again start his journey.

A small and newly painted building serves as the front of the dharamsala that stands between the terminus of casual forays of travellers to the valley and the beginning of a much arduous trek into the depths of the Himalayas for the fervid devotees. The guide bids her goodbye at the doors of the building. He pockets the few coins she places in his hands but does not make those small conversations that mark the end of a short-lived acquaintance. When he leaves, she remembers that he never told her his name – becoming one of hundreds who leave nothing more than an ephemeral mark, destined to be forgotten in the expanse of her time.

She pushes open the doors of the building with no expectations. Since the days of her mother's cruelty, she has shunned decisions as if agency was her biggest enemy. In the face of a painful lack of choices, she finds life to be humble and manageable; its screaming need to ascertain itself recedes with time, and the ebbs and flows of its character become like the cycles of days. She keeps her eyes on the ground, hopping from one eroded stone to another over the river. As long as she doesn't look up, she neither sees nor hears the colossal wall of water that threatens to wash over her. This journey too has ensued because of such non-decisions.

The man who greets her from the sober desk in the otherwise bare room is not the owner of the establishment. His cold, beaten face is small – rather mousey. His nose entirely too prominent on the flushed visage where it rests, and his heart-shaped lips too small to stand against the shadow of the grand feature. She has seen Kailash in the newspapers – the son of a pundit who sacrificed business work that could further their prosperity to comfort a dozen generations, in favour of a calling. Kumar had long contemplated featuring Kailash's pious epiphany. It was odd, perhaps even contemptuous for someone of Kumar's stature to find wealth of similar bulk dispersed into cold air: labour of one's ancestors eschewed for something as plebeian as social work. But Lord Shiva had himself appeared before Kailash in his dreams, and so close to where the fertile waters flowed from His tresses, Kailash did not deem himself esurient enough to ignore serendipity.

She is disappointed to not meet Kailash at the gates of his dharamsala. His rotund face is familiar to her. She has memorized the downturn of his thin mouth, accentuated by the sagging jowls of his cheeks. She knows the shape and cut of the gold-set opal he wears on the third finger of his right hand, and the single, conspicuous chain of gold around his neck. She has sensed in his displays a proud exhibition of the benevolence that the gods have bestowed on him.

The man at the desk – Subodh – does not dally. He ignores the slight disappointment in her pressed mouth and the slow recession of the day's easy joys into those corners she recognizes to be an abyss of forgotten moments of overwhelming rarity. He bows his head deeply and folds his hands close to his heart. His easy nature and friendly smile waver only briefly when she has no answer to his only question. She does not know when her days here will end. She has arrived in the snuggling warmth of this valley like she has alighted at every destination so far. Her mind simply desired serenity, and she let the valley seek her out.

Subodh is still perceptive when he heaves her small bag onto his shoulders. The dharamsala often sees her kind, though women remain fairly uncommon. Perhaps they don't feel the grief of humanity that bends the necks of men or, in their sheltered existence, do not seek the greater truths. In his long time manning his desk that earlier used to lie under a thatched, leaking roof, he has shown the way to several souls of the afflicted kind. They walk in, hunched and crying, and float out the same doors weeks later, their woes of lost money and troubles left behind at the feet of a *shivlinga* made of ice.

He himself had been a kindred man, jaunting through life with those basal passions that so entice a man before destroying their weak mien. There had not been enough liquor to douse his insatiable thirst, nor a woman beautiful enough to be lain with twice. He likely had children wherever he had set foot, but he was now on a journey where worldly attachments were no longer his concern.

She too would be welcomed into Kishore's hearth. But she seems destitute and penniless, and before long, Subodh is convinced she would stand behind him, trudging the bags of another.

✿

Subodh walks her to a small hut at the far edge of the premises. Its walls touch the virgin arboretum beyond, and the spiky leaves of towering rhododendrons threaten to burst through the glass barred window. The open ground, scattered with dozens of similar huts, is wretched and soggy from untimely rains. Her threadbare canvas shoes sink into patches of loosened mud, and when she strains them out, they drag heavily beneath her. Wildflowers and grass wilt, clogged and trampled. Unsaddled horses and mules graze about the ground, sniffing through their stocky noses for areas that have not suffered from rains or feet.

An ecstatic dog runs excited and largely ignored circles around them.

The valley here clears up to reveal sheer faces of denuded mountains. She peers over her shoulder to get her bearings, the welcoming building of brick and cement left behind in its singular display of modernity. It stands small and feeble in the cupped palm of the mountains – earlier so grand and solid, now no more than an ant in a field.

The hut, however, is dilapidated. The façade of prosperity drops like a misleading veil. Subodh rests her luggage under a crackling switchboard and, telling her the time for supper, walks away with the same straight-backed composure that she has come to associate with inherent self-assurance. Beyond the barred windows, there is only darkness. The forest thickens, abandoning the cheerfully radiant and spacious spread of chir for the thicker, congested girths of deodar. Past the younger frontier of trees, she will one day exert herself till the break of dawn. But for now, she pays it no mind.

The deplorable state of the hut, which would have disheartened any other, fills her with comfort. It is a habit from a past so long forgotten that it could have been some story she read about a miserable character. In that house, dust would settle on books and radios and sacks of grain merely hours after cleaning. She would twirl and dance in the halos of light that filtered in through gaps between walls and holes in shades, the spinning motes her companions.

In the hut, sunlight shies away from the critters that burrow into its old wood. The single incandescent bulb lights the yellowed pillow and bedsheet. A forlorn wooden desk and chair that remind her of school stand abandoned under the window. In a dark corner, there is a peti. She fishes out the nutcracker from the bottom of her bag and slides it into the peti, where it will lie until some curious pilgrim finds it in the daylight hours, years later.

TEN

Where the broadest peaks of the mountain range stand tall, the first rays of the sun have already begun to bathe the summits with orange halos. The ancient snow gleams with an ethereal light, and from those surfaces, clouds rise like plumes of smoke from a distant chimney. Songbirds harp their songs early, their playful babble heralding another day in the heart of the valley.

The dharamsala will rise only a few moments later – the kitchen women to prepare a steaming breakfast of khichdi, the priests to bless pilgrims on their resumed journey, and soon, the pilgrims themselves. They will awaken to the displeasing tinkling of the temple bells. They will dress hurriedly, their faces drawn downwards by cold, uncomfortable sleep and a peculiar inner desolation. A man will throw open the doors of the hut, and a stream of people will pour out. They will line up close by and urinate into the nearest bushes. Meanwhile, the women will quickly pull down the trousers and skirts of their young children, and hastily yell at them to piss and defecate in a corner of the hut. They will leave soon anyway. If and when the time arises, they will cover their noses with the ends of their saris and skirt, go to the back of their huts and do their own business.

But long before these flurries of activity ring the valley into commotion, with the first spot of orange on the peaks of the mountains, workers arise from dilapidated huts set against a large outcropping several long yards away from the lodgings of the pilgrims. These are the homes of sweepers and cleaners – manual scavengers, who begin their day by surveying the earth between forested colonnades to dig makeshift lavatories. Loamy soil littered with decaying foliage is ideal. Mounds appearing to leak with thick sludge are best avoided.

The figure of a tall man appears. His face is dark in the shadows, though his silhouette cuts lean from labour and hardship. Closer to the gods, the hierarchies are stricter, and he is expected to move as a ghost. He catches a glimpse of the sunlit mountaintop. He is late in waking today. Soon, summons will arrive from Subodh's men to carry away waste from the now-emptied huts. There will be splatters and streaks on the walls, left in a hurry to be closer to some god who is perhaps not as fastidious as he. The pilgrims never inform anyone of their activities, and after all these years, the sweepers are still surprised to find remnants of their devotion.

Kailash will be the last to wake, much after those lowly managers have opened the doors of the dharamsala, several hours after the pilgrims have set off on their journey after breakfast, and almost a lifetime after the earth has been dug and the walls of the huts scrubbed clean of urine and solid waste.

The stench in the nearby forest is rather unbearable. One would expect that the waving leaves and blooming flowers – the woody scent of maturing cones, the petrichor of rained-on soil and the more mystical fragrance of the quiet hum of the forest – would mask that of human waste. But it never does. The rainwater worsens the odour as the waste seeps to the surface and certain clearings reek of festering sweat. It is hard work. One of isolation and segregation. If he happens to walk about the premises when the dharamsala is at its most gregarious, people skirt around him, arcing a long radius from him as if his skin wafts the fetid smell of their excretions in the forest.

He often wonders if it would have been better if he was born into a slightly higher strata – if instead of a shovel, he carried a broom; if instead of carrying away faeces, he swept away soil. The work, however, is a welcome and anticipated distraction from the thoughts that steal sleep from his eyes and relief from his limbs.

Their home is young – a new name remarks its archaic existence. A renewed identity boils the young blood, but his brother, not even in his second decade and with no more than a few tendrils of hair above his lip, is simply expected as a Dalit to let the flood of nationalism wash him into the midst of a distant eastern war. The last time he sees his brother is when in shorts and shirt of khakhi, he arrives at Kailash's doors. They are gathered at the landfill that Kailash has instructed to be dug wider every three months that the dharamsala is in business. The hill is slowly hollowing, its innards nothing but plastic and mismatched rags, its heart beating with the incendiary fluids of new technology.

'The landfill has thinned the walls of the hill, Pundit Ji,' his young brother says. The boys stand looking at each other, childish mischief in their eyes.

'There can be landslides,' he says before leaving.

One last look at his brother. A promise to resume their boyish games once again.

A missive arrives in lieu of him.

✿

Through the haze of sleep in her eyes and the glue that mars her vision this early in the morning, she does not notice the figure of the man in the dark. She knows of the sweepers and the diggers. She has seen them move in the earliest hours of dawn, much earlier, when it can still be called night – their activities expected to blend into the dark. If it wasn't for the fitful sleep that leaves her grumbling and turning in her small cot, she wouldn't have taken notice. It is not usual for those who sully in their wake to care for those who walk into their refuse.

Within the layers of her mind, the nutcracker is antecedent to her disquietude. She feels its weight between her shoulders, in the palm of her hands, and between her breasts, where it rests, densely pressing into her bones. She finds it hard to draw breaths, and her dreams, already harried, toe the line between wakefulness and slumber till distantly familiar figures materialize in her hut.

The squatters' spot that serves as the dharamsala's outhouse begins to mill with activity when the first rays of the sun reach the valley. With the passage of time, each row of trees stinks with the excreta of its patron – one sentry for each. The first time she visits, bare-bottomed women and children stare at her going about her ablutions. She learns to time the activities of the sweepers, whose slow and burdened walk back to their huts marks a small window in which she can relieve herself without the curious eyes of those who seem to harbour a masked obsession with ordure.

On days when sheets of rain obscure her vision of the valley, she instead times herself with the arrival of a white bird. It takes cover in the dense and spiky thick of the rhododendron that hugs her window. Sheltered from the rain, it spreads dew on its wings and feathers. In the brilliant silver light of the moon, a part of its beautiful white plumage stands out in the gloom of the otherwise morbid day.

The white bird is the mysterious bird of a man's memoirs she had read as a child – a hunter and later a conservator. Divided by several decades, she nonetheless feels a timeless proximity with him. Larger than a kite but smaller than a vulture, and brilliant in its white plumage but not an egret, songbird-like in its nocturnal melody, but not of the same family, and with a trailing train like a bird of paradise, but not quite tropical. He had believed it to be the last one of its kind, and now she finds its solitary asylum in her rhododendron to be a confirmation of his suspicions.

The white bird arrives in the midst of pouring heavens, and in the short while in which it has groomed itself with beads of scintillating raindrops on its gorgeous plume, the rain subsides. The bird's erratic departure soon after marks her cue. The sweepers have retired into the marginal warmth of their hearths. But the sweeper today is late, and when she walks into the forest, she runs into the man who, encumbered with thoughts of his lost brother, does not notice her.

The man mumbles. Short, bothered sentences – of his abandoned mother in a village far away; of times with his young brother, running into an elephant shed to play with Ilavati; of a body left behind in faraway lands that he has never heard of. In the shadows, she can still see the lines on his forehead and the morose downturn of his mouth. The shovel he carries drags behind him in the soft dirt, uprooting stalks of grass from their roots. She extends a hand in his direction, gently brushing his strong arm. He shudders only briefly but walks away, unaware of the tender sprout of sympathy that is extended to him.

Her life, which previously resembled that of an elusive hermit, now slowly takes shape into that of a rat. Interactions, formerly tolerated, are avoided at all costs. She is skittish and alert. Rather vigilant, in her opinion. But perhaps more paranoid. The sweeper is the first in many days to elicit a semblance of a positive response from her. She sees in his posture her own burdens. They are not of an immediate or physical kind. They do not settle with the massaging in of a salve, nor with the sympathetic words of a stranger to appease the injury. They gnaw and tear; meaty chunks that fly large distances, essential parts of souls that could be gathered, if only the bearer of these wounds knew whence they land.

But this sympathy, and likely some empathy, lasts only a few moments. She is not an oasis of pity, and however much that wells, it must be spent on herself. The sweeper appears slouching deeper into the bowels of the earth, but she has housed her sorrows longer. She has nurtured them for years – watered them with her body's moisture and watched as they blossomed into wilted flowers. Her misery, shaped and sheltered, has been her most constant and cordial companion. There is no room for others.

In this dharamsala, such miseries sprout like wild grass between cobblestones. People's groans and moans, their maladies and desires, their hopes and losses buzz in the wind like aphids in harvest season. Asters and geraniums still grow. The green carpet that shrouds the undulating valley still thrives with lushness. The sun-kissed snowy peaks of the distant mountains still gleam in the day. She wonders how long before these majestic troughs and crests crumble to the destructive horrors of man. How long before the wails and pleas of their believers shame the gods into action?

She, however, cannot avoid the crowd of the dharamsala for long. The first day, she lets the dingy, ill-lit air of her hut press down on her. Bright noonday light spreads a sheet of blinding yellow from under the door. She is unfamiliar with the dry chill of the mountains, and her legs ache from yesterday's labours. The thick blankets deliciously soothe the pain, and she rubs her cheeks into their downy-soft fabric. But Subodh wakes her eventually. His sickening smile never fades, nor do his shoulders show signs of relief when she opens the door. It is evident, though, that her long absence could be considered concerning, a potential scandal that the revered dharamsala and its stalwart owner would rather avoid.

She hides when opportunity presents her with such morsels. Subodh is a pest, a stubborn leech that cannot be shaken off. He hounds her with absurd questions that he expects no answers to. He is rather thin, of the sickly sort; the kind only managed by years of dependence on something that slowly sucks out all gentle roundness of the body. She has seen it on Mrs Pradhan, whose bloated joints against her spindly frame make her caricaturistic – a parody of what her sunset beauty could have been. Before that, she had seen her uncle, his drawn-in cheeks stretched tightly over the fragile bones of his face. He had large, protruding eyes, much like her father, and so afflicted with an unnatural gauntness, he was demonic.

Subodh still waits, his eerily smiling eyes fixed on her face. A pause of no more than five heartbeats, not enough to make sense of his query, let alone to deliver a comprehensive answer. The first few times, she relents, falls for the ruse. He is showing her the dharamsala – the kitchens where women shout and yell across the room, their bodies obscured by the steam rising from containers so large, they could boil a beast in them. She learns that her hut was previously a broom-shed and all the other huts were packed with several cots. There are three temples on the premises, though throughout her stay, she never visits to greet the deities inside.

Subodh is, as expected, not much concerned with the terrain – the weighty florets of the primula held on a tender stalk, the apollos of nature. A scimitar babbler hobbles ahead of them, its white eyebrows comical across its small head. These are birds and flowers of her childhood. Her memory jogs. Pictures from her father's gifts prod at her mind, pleading to rise to the surface. Her mother's words – 'A curious mind is rewarded by Ganpati Ji and lives an adventurous life' – blend into the absurdity of Subodh's question.

'If man's purpose is to build and acquire, then why do they so often find themselves weeping at their mother's bosom?' he asks. His voice is meditative. Practised. He has asked this question several times, honed the answer to his satisfaction until it was like balm to the pilgrim's wounds. Kailash might stay in his home with sloping roofs, but on these grounds, Subodh is the owner of people's miseries.

'Yes, man by nature is a creature of collection. He must build and he must hoard. But what he must collect is not material riches. It is not the fearful admiration of several, nor the kind of power that leaves him alone. It is love. It is generosity. He must build a community, guide the straying hearts of those who are as lost as he. He must adore those who spit at him. Console those who rage at him. He must become the harbour for beaten souls who wash up onto him. This is what he must acquire.'

With time, Subodh's philosophical façade drops. There are no more curiosities that require his deep thoughts, and whatever he has found to be the truth ceases to be enough to converse with her, who has now been at the dharamsala for one week. She finds his new reticence to be freeing. The clatter of activity at the dharamsala follows her around instead.

She stands in groups that wait with steaming plastic cups of tea. The men keep their eyes on the mules being loaded with their belongings. They shout harsh words and cheap sounds at porters for fear of their clothes and donations. The women squat in circles, tightening their woollen *topas* and mufflers around themselves. They have come for the blessing of a son, for their new peanut business to succeed, for the security of a government job, for the recovery of an ailing mother, for a good and fortunate husband, for the acceptance of a love union, for absolution of sin in the fading years of an existence. She learns that they rarely come to pay reverence to God Himself.

The noise does not follow her into the forest that rises to the hills from the walls of the valley. She travels into it, where fallen logs, pregnant with activity, bring the woods to themselves. She waits for the brilliant blue of a flycatcher as it snaps at an unsuspecting insect mid-air. She follows the sluggish path of millipedes that curl into tight coils at the shaking ground beneath the pads of their innumerable legs.

Her breath hitches at the arrival of a nutcracker on its long legs. Its silver beak like the whistling blade of an axe. Its neck and stomach like a patch of flowering cotton pods. Its awkward, odd cawing an anathema to the slick, back-combed crown. When it hops into a spot of sunlight, the bird shimmers like Mrs Pradhan's nutcracker. She turns and leaves.

Now, when Subodh harries her, it is about money. He materializes from behind huts, squats nearby during lunchtime when her fingers are buried in her dal chawal, when she is patting the soft, curved backs of mules that huff contentedly at her.

'It is a dharamsala only in name, madamji,' he says. The leery smile stays.

ELEVEN

Afterwards, when her money runs out, Subodh knocks an ear-splitting beat on her door and takes her to Kailash's house. She does not expect to be allowed to live in her broom-shed without making regular payments for the shelter and food that barely nourishes her, but she does not wish to work either. She has found fulfilment in her wanderings at the edge of the forest. In a small diary, she has pressed several flowers she has collected from the muddy ground. She recognizes daisies and poppies and asters – the bulging centre of an anemone, the drooping azure of wolfsbane, the deceptive hood of the cobra lily. But there are several that her memories cannot place. After her uncle, there was no appeal in the mundane, bottomless expanse of the world. The colours of sunset became drab. The jujube that had fed the child for several summers was now thorny and unpleasant to look at.

The abandonment of the pursuit of the natural world left holes in her knowledge. But now those wonders were glimmering in front of her eyes. They send cold caressing winds in the morning, beckoning her into the forest. On separate pages, she presses a small yellow flower, a creeping stem of red leaves and a bunch of delicate whorls of a purple cluster. She has no names for them yet, but she leaves an empty page for each. In the valley where one cannot walk without trampling dozens of flowers, she once again finds the spark.

Kailash's rectangular house, painted a blinding white and adorned with swastikas on either side of the doors, is ill-suited to the habitat in which it resides. It is too concrete, too stone and cement, too sharp and outlined to belong in the rugged shapelessness of the mountains. At the threshold, she decides she will soon sell the nutcracker. Perhaps the city where pilgrims and adventurers alight – the last destination before the journey into the mountain could only be taken on foot – is not the ideal place to sell something of its heft. The rubies alone would command a great, comfortable price. The simple emeralds on both handles are the size of her thumbnail. She could lead a splendid life in the broom-shed, waking early to follow the pheasants into the sleeping woods.

Kailash himself does not resemble the shadowed black-and-white picture that accompanied the full-page ads *The Narrator* ran in each edition for seven months. He sits on a wooden sofa, his thick legs clothed in white pants, shaking anxiously. A pundit, sitting on the floor close to him, reads him a *paath*. She and Subodh have arrived at the wrong time. Kailash keeps his eyes closed, sometimes shaking his head in acquiescence, other times dropping his head lower in shame at the pundit's words. She has never seen a man so pious – and the display seems comical. An appearance to settle the soul even when no one is watching.

The pundit takes his slow leave. He gathers his books and leaflets in a red cloth, carefully ties a rope around it and lifting his large body with a straining hand on his knee, hobbles out the door – much like Leela will hobble in, a few moments later.

Kailash turns out to be a cautious man. He has long carried a prudent image – one of a man given to spiritual impulses but following through on them with the circumspect manners of a businessman. It is not uncommon at his dharamsala for individuals of a certain affliction to make it their home. Subodh was one. Jagdish, who is now as good as his right hand, was another. The worlds beyond the valley are tiring and draining, and Kailash admires the grandeur of a higher need that they bring to the dharamsala. Their stories make for good headlines too, and in the years since he discovered there is more comfort and splendour in a life in the shadow of faith, he has not spent more than a few monies attracting people to his rather unusual dharamsala.

He cannot yet call it an *ashram*, though he wishes for nothing else. He would name it after his father: Swami Bhairo Das Ashram. There will be a large auditorium where pilgrims will meditate and chant. There will be *baithaks* and movements. Famous foreigners will grace the front building he has built in anticipation of his dreams. But he now lacks only one element for Swami Bhairo Das Ashram. He has no godman, no medium who has renounced the material dictates and deeper sorrows of life in search of incorporeal pleasures. He does, however, have Leela. The people at the dharamsala call her Leela Ma. She reads charts and palms till patrons sigh with relief and sob at the tenderness and warmth that emanates from her. Her childlike face and sympathetic eyes enfold seekers like the discerning embrace of a mother. But she is still a child – only sixteen – and pregnant with his first child. He cannot yet shroud her in a plain red sari or put her face on a poster to be hung at the front building.

Kailash does not pry like Subodh. In his perfunctory questions, she senses a motive similar to Mrs Pradhan's. 'What do you do? Where did you grow up? When did you arrive here?' He has no wish to know her, nor does he find her lingering a cause for concern. Yet, Kailash Vishram Kendra remains a business, and those unable to line its coffers must find another purpose.

'My wife is very young,' Kailash says. He does not look into her eyes. He avoids those of Subodh completely, whose animated countenance has long since unsettled him.

'She does not have many companions her age.' He sighs. Leela is not given to quibble. She is not passive either. Leela is simply content with her lot. But he has once lost a wife to the emptiness that comes with a profound lack of an empathetic ear, and he is fearful of the infinite time at the dharamsala that lies ahead for Leela.

'She is with child. Only two more months. I worry she might be lonely,' he says. Kailash finally looks up at her. A rounded face of resignation. She sits unmoving, as if waiting for retribution. A feigned composure even more upsetting than Subodh's latent, prurient gaze.

'Leela has seen you around the premises. She believes you like nature. She does too, and perhaps the two of you can spend some time together. It will remove a weight from my shoulders and give you reason to stay here longer as well,' he concludes.

There is no request in Kailash's words. No choice. He has simply stated a fact in so many words. She knows of Leela Ma. The pilgrims talk of her, sometimes wait a day longer to consult with her. The journey further north is eased by her words. The fears and dreams that people hoard close to their hearts become lighter to bear once they have heard affirmations from her.

On cue, Leela hobbles in, supporting her growing belly with

a hand. She thinks Kailash's wife is perhaps too young. Her skin is only lightly marked, as if adolescence is yet to unleash its complete fury on her. Except for the jutting roundness of her growing child, she is small and narrow. Her stature is that of a child, and her bones still in a state of development. It's her face that is jarring – that of an old monkish contentment and safety. When Leela sees her regarding her carefully, she smiles. It makes her uncomfortable, this feigned familiarity, as if Leela has known her before in some distant time. As if in another life, they were sisters. As if once regarded, Leela knows her heart.

She moves in her place as Leela shuffles in. Kailash and Subodh wait for her to sit but do not extend a hand. Impatience rises in the room. Leela's condition, now a matter of her otherworldly affinity, is also cause for much annoyance. Her frailty is of concern, but there are no complaints from Leela herself.

No more words are exchanged between Kailash and her. Subodh too seems ready to take his leave. It will soon be time to open the doors of the dharamsala, and he has been preparing for his philosophical benediction since he woke up at the break of dawn. It is Leela who says the parting words, meant less to conclude this gathering and more to mark the beginning of another.

'Those flowers you don't know – they are vajradanti, jungli ajwain and amli. But do not go too deep into the forest in search of more wonders. There are many beasts hidden within.'

✿

It has been many weeks since she has witnessed the unyielding cogs of society turning and churning. The dharamsala's grounds are not a good measure of her previous reality. She yearns to get a foot back in civilization – to see a man fix his tie on his way to work, a woman turn out the last of an overused lipstick before beginning her day, the cacophonous curiosities and games of uniform-clad children carrying their aspirations on their backs to school. From the entrance that she had walked into this part of her life, she now exits.

She will return early, she thinks. But for a few moments, she wants distance from Leela's kind face, who follows her around like a smitten dog. Her shifted balance makes her forays into the deeper parts of the forest precarious, though Leela insists on accompanying her from the moment her shape appears at the doors of the broom-shed, spied from several yards away. The first few times, she tests Leela's limit – walking unspeaking into the woods, where trunks hug closer and closer, and to her fallen log of oak where the spotted nutcracker visits. They climb rock-littered grazing grounds up into the thick. Her feet sometimes catch on overgrown roots and loosened mud left behind after midnight rains. At the top of the hill, the entrance to the forest awaits. She turns around to admire the scattered huts of the dharamsala in the distance, now nothing more than children's toys. Leela is only halfway through. She bends to use her hands on tricky steps, and her stomach squeezes grotesquely between her breasts and knees. When Leela reaches her, she is huffing with the excitement of a tired pup. Her face is red with exertion, but her eyes wide with exhilaration.

Leela's enthusiastic acceptance of her reluctant company rankles at her. Resigned to her fate and carrying a smidgen of concern for the young mother's state, she is confined to walk around the perimeter of the dharamsala. There are no discoveries to be made on the trampled ground. They often run into dung pellets of mules and mounds of garbage sparkling with packets of paan masala. Leela begins to drag her into her home, where the two sit in silence, surrounded by displays of new wealth – in the knitted cloth over the transistor that only works a few hours a day, in paisley bedsheets and sofa covers, and shell curtains above Leela's bedroom door.

The city is a bustling port of frantic devotion. It isn't so much a centre of industrial enterprise that occupies her mind in the several hours between the dharamsala and here. It is astir with a manic surrender to faith. In the heart of the city, breaths mingle and bodies collide. She apologizes to a woman running with a handful of burning lamps. Behind her, another woman yells at her to watch where she is going. The lamps need to be safely delivered into the waters of the river.

For several hours, she walks aimlessly around the city, sometimes standing at the edge of a cliff to watch the flurry of activity at the banks, which never quietens. Shirtless priests prepare for their evenings along the straining bodies of washerwomen – dirt of one kind mingling with another at the fringes of the river. Other times, she chooses the narrow streets in the heart of the city, old tennis balls occupied in games of cricket flying over her head, the stream of garbage falling from a higher floor, missed by a breath. The city sometimes regurgitates her into a different world – one bustling with hippies and spiritual seekers of different nationalities. Here, several tongues blend into each other, and in the cacophony that ensues, she finds the lack of comprehension to be an odd comfort. It is in these corners that she finds Gustav and his friends.

✿

Gustav is tall and dangerously thin. Emaciated. His long limbs are a study in anatomy – taut tendons, swollen green veins, protruding balls of shoulders, elbows and knees, more skin than flesh. The insides of his arms are bruised purple. When they embrace and kiss for the first time, he tastes of rot and foliage. It overrides her fears that set her heart racing and drumming in her chest. With time, she lets herself forget all others. The intimacy comes to mean Gustav – intertwined with his snaking limbs and the assortment of his smells. Scents of the earth, which she doesn't particularly mind. He knows only a few words in English, just enough to fill the silence between passions. Never enough to kindle conjugal hopes.

Afterwards, he lies on his back, his eyes fixed on some riveting squall on the ceiling that only he perceives. He speaks in German; his voice flowing in a level baritone. Low and controlled though it is, he speaks at length as if reciting some beloved passage from a book or proselytizing her with his scriptures. She presses her ear onto his bare, hairy chest. At certain sounds, his chest purrs and rumbles. She hopes that the proximity to its origins would forever etch the sounds into her memory.

Gustav's propensity for anxious, unceasing movement, however, is surprising. It's remarkable, she thinks, after she has seen him rise once again out of the punishing daze of morphine and go about his mundane routines as if the dead weight of what flows in his blood is not trying to walk him to his sleep. He often stumbles, stills and sways on his feet, as if dozing after a tiring day. But Gustav must always be doing something.

Clutter from the previous day's gathering is cleared within hours. Ashtrays of paper and crystal and porcelain are emptied out the window. It is the neighbourhood's dumpyard, and

Gustav, François and Anita have been here long enough to feel at home with its customs. He collects chillums and pipes, tubes and bubblers, and sits down cross-legged. On the floor before him, he spreads the assembled accoutrements. So begins the arduous task of poking, blowing and rinsing with a fervid concentration. The only true face of manic, pious devotion she has ever seen. Sheets are retucked, chairs replaced, windows thrown wide open to air the rooms, dishes scrubbed with cheap powder. François and Anita have not yet awoken.

Other times, Gustav reads. Mostly in German, sometimes in French and once in Bengali for amusement. The titles are unfamiliar, unreadable, but she mouths the writers' names – easier to pronounce for nomenclatural propinquity. Gustav Landauer, von Arnim, de Beauvoir. He never sits or reclines while reading; it is neither a chore to be done disheartened, nor a bromidic hobby to be partaken in if and when time allows. It is his education that he has taken on himself. He briskly paces the room, his neck bent awkwardly and his otherwise scrawny arm holding the book with the sure stability of a surgeon. Every few minutes, he reads a passage aloud for an undefined period of time, and thus having found his focus, continues to read quietly.

Gustav is not a good lover. Perhaps in some other time, he must have been attentive, gentle and caring. Now his drug-addled days leave him disoriented and irritable, until he gives up quickly and hurries to his pouch of needle and spoon. The lack of linguistic commonality chafes at them both. Sometimes the two lie in bed and repeat the words of the other. *Herzschlag. Pitambar. Unzufriedenheit. Siamese. Deesee.* These tender attempts at understanding are, however, not enough.

When she invites him to come stay with her at the dharamsala, he smiles at her with uncomprehending blankness.

✿

She spends most of her time at Gustav's apartment above a small grocery shop. Compared to the rank dinginess of Mrs Pradhan's rental and the crawling chill of her hut at the dharamsala, the apartment is flooded with light and the racket of a city in motion during the daytime, and the heavy, somnolent retirement of night. The hours spent with Leela, though at times less than a fortnight old, fade and smudge like portraits of a generation ago.

She still frequently takes the journey between the valley and the city. Though Gustav's unspoken affection has, for now, sequestered the noise in her mind, the fleeting nature of their association agonizes her. It is an itch she worries over until it wounds, festers and scabs. She pulls at it and begins again. The broom-shed at the dharamsala is a home in ways that Gustav's will one day fail to be, and this knowledge shakes her awake and sets her onto the curved road along the river.

This journey, which once took her an entire morning, she now covers with the nimble feet of a mountain goat. Rest stops selling tea and snacks greet her by name. A dog, she calls Monty, meets her on a narrow stretch and walks with her a short distance, till they reach a clump of sundry shrubs and bushes lively with the playful chirrups of tits. She and Monty rest a while, tracking the aimless path of the birds, until Monty, perhaps reminded of his duty to accompany another, under another name, bids her goodbye. She waits until his wagging tail disappears along the sinuous trail.

She believes it must be enough if she is spotted by a few at the dharamsala every day. Going into or coming out of her hut. Only one would be an apparition. Several would be cause for intervention. Subodh becomes a constant, but her hurried steps never allow him a chance to enquire. If, on her way, she runs into Jagdish, she marks the day to be of exceptional luck. He is trusted and revered, and his words carry weight like Subodh's never could. Sometimes, she stands outside the large doors of the kitchen, laughing and exchanging stories with the kitchen women. If she is early in her arrival, she helps boys saddle horses and mules. One time, she spots Leela from a distance, and doesn't return to the valley for two days. Leela now stands with both her hands on her belly.

Gustav's apartment – the very harbour of quietude in the daytime – becomes a haven for those who prefer the anonymity of night in the evenings. In the dimness of hanging lights, and the frequent spark of a lit match or lighter, it lifts itself from the theological dominion of the city and occupies its space in youthful ether. The painted images of Ganesh and Parvati on the wall across the grocery store, the begging bowls of the homeless and the lepers, the thundering march of devotees to the ghats, the clamour of ringing bells during *aarti*, the inviting sing-song chants of pundits, and claims of great fortune in exchange of donations to temples, become identities of a distant city in her imagination.

There are too many faces, too many names to remember. The rooms thicken with bodies until she cannot see Gustav's familiar figure. Separated by language, she is left out of games of cards and drug-numbed discussions that impassion several groups at a time. She once again feels like a child faced with boundless variables. She avoids the writhing bodies of dancing couples and the spots near windows where cigarettes go off in dozens. It reminds her of Aarav, and she pushes her face into the fumes of incense that François keeps burning throughout the day at his door. The heady smell of marijuana – that feels like musk on Gustav – crawls its heaving way into the back of her throat. Every night, she waits for Gustav to find her.

✿

One day, she finds the apartment empty. Not just unoccupied but abandoned. The doors are locked, and when she pries open the windows beside them, the apartment looks stripped of life. The faded blue sofa is still under the windows on the other side. Two wooden cabinets still rest against the wall of the front room. Some of their drawers are thrown open. The desk where Gustav kept his volumes of revolutionary literature is still hidden partly behind a corner. But the books are gone. The absence of Anita's Afghan on the sofa has left a dustless spot on it. François's incense has burned through and not been replaced.

Downstairs, she approaches the middle-aged woman who mans the grocery shop. 'Do you know where they are?' Her body is sheltered behind plastic boxes of candies and curtains of jarda and *elaichi*. Two girls – her daughters – regard her with curiosity. They have perhaps seen her with Gustav, their hands linked. 'Left a few hours ago. Seemed in a hurry,' the woman says, never looking up from her register.

'Did they say anything?'

She is irritated by the woman's curt responses. It is her family's building, and her concealed answers seem abstruse. Wouldn't they know where their tenants had disappeared to?

The woman doesn't respond. Instead, she lifts a plastic box and dumps the wrapped candies in front of her. It is the morning of inventory. Finally, the two girls shake their heads – as much in answer to her query as to prod her to move along.

It could not have been more than six or seven hours since she had sneaked away from Gustav's bed. He was clammy and sweaty, like always. She had thought, in a couple of hours, he would awake, shaking towards his pouch. Now, it is still the peak of the day. Several people are yet to dip into the river. The shops that had closed after the morning prayers have their shutters down, retired for an early lunch and afternoon rest. It will be several hours before the preparations for the evening aarti begin.

She walks up to the hill where a Shiva temple overlooks the confluence of several rivers. At these hours, when the sun transforms the surface of still waters to mercury, the cold stones of the temple are a respite for many – but the open courtyard is empty. Why did Gustav leave so suddenly? Why did he not leave her a note? In what language, she thinks, what words could he use for such an abrupt departure from her life?

Under the shimmering surface of the rivers, the water is mucky and disgusting. Where the river smashes against rocks, the churn sometimes throws up pieces of plastic and sludgy debris. She too is one of such dregs expelled from the turgid flow of people's lives. Her mother, her brothers and sisters – now Gustav.

By the time she reaches the dharamsala, it is past sunset. She covers the last narrow leg before the mouth of the valley in darkness. Monty and she sit at their spot for hours. He rests his hands on his stick-like legs and watches her with sympathetic eyes. It is she who leaves eventually. Monty watches her unsure back disappear and retires for the day.

The dharamsala is alive with the anticipation of dinner, the warmth and comfort of the huts briefly forsworn for the burning food. A single light burns in the distance. In her broom-shed, Leela sits on a chair, her eyes upturned towards the stars, and waits for her to return.

TWELVE

'Don't think Kailash did not notice your absence,' Subodh says the next day. She is brushing a mule that has just undertaken a return journey from the temple in the hills beyond. Its eyes close leisurely, even if he shakes on his tired legs.

'Only a fool wouldn't have,' she says. Subodh, in her time away, has taken up the habit of chewing tobacco. He retracts his thick lip and shovels some into his mouth now. The unnerving smile returns again, and the corners of it fill with red juice.

'I didn't tell him of it,' Subodh says. There is some suggestion of salacity in his words today. The pride of triumph over his basal desires has once again been replaced with a nature that lies dormant. His esoteric sagacity only lasts so long a season.

She doesn't think Subodh to be a tattle. He desires – no, expects – something from her. His remissions are not unusual, and she recognizes it the first time she sees it. But Subodh's masked threats are pointless. There has been no reprimand from Kailash. When she met him in the morning, he only asked after her health. His careful, avuncular concern was an extension of Leela's sororal love towards her. From where it stems, she can't tell.

Leela held her close the night before. At the door of the broom-shed, she didn't cry or weep, and Leela's protruding belly sat awkwardly between the two. She was not soothed or surprised by her actions – the girl has become Leela Ma for this same proclivity to reserved troubles, which she perceives with exceptional love. She, however, for once let it be. When it was time for Leela to return, Kailash sent a man, and the two walked back together in companionable silence.

Till the early hours of the morning, she slept peacefully. The resentment was calmed by the lingering sensation of Leela's hands on her back and head. When she wakes, the sound of pattering rain keeps her from falling back asleep. The window is a flowing sheet of water, and the white bird's silhouette has not yet arrived to mark the soon-clear skies. Some of the rhododendrons sway in the storm and send eerie shadows into her broom-shed.

She has not seen herself in a mirror in long. When she does, she imagines a formless figure will stare back at her. In place of its eyes, a well of murky blankness will peer and enquire. From that misty distance, she wonders, if there will be something to see at all. In her wake, she realizes, she has relinquished not just material possessions but some quintessential kernels that keep one stitched together.

As a child, her grandfather instilled in her a habit of keeping diaries. When her sister fell asleep, she pulled a stool from under their bed and slid it towards the window where light from a streetlamp fell into their room. The stool was too heavy for her young arms, and she covered the screeching legs with layers of rags that she borrowed from her mother. In those diaries, she did not have much to say about the now. She placed little value on the recent – there was not much space for the mundanity of her mother running out with knives when she heard the wheel of the knife-grinder outside their gate, nor for the man who arrived with a bellowing call to sell his teeth-whitening powder. Her wants and needs were larger; her world of wonder too massive for the street that began with the squalor of a small-time dairy and ended with the unquiet house of a divorced history teacher. She would write, she would see the great creations of man with her own eyes, she would bask in the glorious existence of nature.

My poetry will one day make an elderly man weep on his desk with adoration.

A boy will clip my words from a magazine to serenade his lover.

My mother and I will sway and glide in the halls of the Palace of Versailles.

The shadow in the mirror is a shell of that child, its outline lying on a bed in a remote dharamsala, its essence floating between the dairyman and the teacher. In the diary she has recently abandoned, she writes, 'The artists' liberties show in the departure from convention. In the snaking vines of the frescoes, there are often subjects that diverge from the motif. A cluster of grapes hides a frog, a detailed depiction of battle is interrupted by a Rolls Royce ...' Words that neither swell the chest with emotion, nor curl the toes of a loved woman.

She turns away from the window beyond which lie those yearnings and longings of an unfamiliar child. In her disturbed sleep, Gustav's partly shaved head pants close to her ear. The long earring he wears tickles her cheek. She raises her hand to slide it over his cropped stubble, but her fingers grab a handful of curly black hair. When Gustav raises his head, it is with the strained aggression of Aarav, before morphing into the gaunt face of her uncle.

✿

With Gustav too now only a part of her memories, even her forays into the forest and the simple menial occupations at the dharamsala fill no more than a few hours of her day. The broom-shed lost its charm the night her dreams tainted the warmth of Gustav's arms with the odorous presence of Aarav and her uncle. At night, she kicks away the comforter that had soothed many aches in her early days in the valley. Now the fabric itches; she sweats and grumbles under its ugly weight.

On the hardest of days, the succour of darkened rooms and turned backs gives way to the fatalistic leanings of the mind. She tosses and turns, her shoulders and back aching with disuse; her neck curled towards her shoulder from her long supine hours. One morning, she wakes and, in a daze, walks towards Kailash's house. A line of mules, followed by bleary-eyed pilgrims, crosses the grounds on the way to their next destination. A few men at the back walk unsteadily, their eyes heavy and cheeks swollen with crapulous disorientation. The kitchen women sit and chatter on the stairs, having their first meals after feeding hundreds. Behind them, the large containers still steam in the kitchen.

It is still rather early. The valley's indigo slumber has given way to sharp lines and colours, but the distant figures still lie in shadows. A lamp is alight on Kailash's patio, but fails to send its glow into the slowly crawling daylight. She expects the doors to be closed – for Leela, Kailash and his mother to be withdrawn in their early domestic activities. But the door is ajar. Leela sits on the sofa, her face only slightly drawn with the remnants of sleep and the growing demands of her body. She moves the needles delicately and deftly between swollen fingers – socks for her unborn child.

It is the first time she has sought Leela of her own accord. The young woman smells of soap and incense. The aura of smoky sandalwood around Leela tugs at her heart; not-so-distant days now blurred around the edges, the faces of Gustav and his friends already losing their sharpness. Leela pats the cushion beside her. 'I have been waiting,' she says.

'I have been away,' she responds.

Leela does not press her further. In her slowly thinning face, she sees guilt. Resignation and resentment. Her disordered actions arise from a turmoil within. Leela has waited calmly for a companion – one she did not know she needed till recently – to fill her laborious days, and now that she has arrived on her own – though wearied and indifferent – she does not wish to press on wounds that might sequester her into her hut again.

Leela is an effusive creature, shunning silences that she refuses to fill with her own disquietude. Leela is only minutely affected by the condition of her body – showing the discomfort through strained breaths and grunts on exerting movements, and ill-timed gaseous expulsions. But Leela is simply too exuberant, too young to trouble herself with what is beyond her grasp. 'You are still too young to birth a child,' she says, one day. It is an unfounded concern. She has been with Leela for only a few hours, and it is scrutiny, rather than apprehension over her new companion's fate, that brings the question to her mind.

'Am I not too deep into it now to be worrying?' Leela says.

Leela's penchant for rhetoric is first vexing, then trying, finally amusing. It becomes a sport between the two. They lie in Leela's bed and beguile their time, each query increasingly risible.

'It is rather cold today,' she says.

'Was it not rather cold yesterday?' Leela replies.

'Chagan's mule kicked him in the chest today.'

'Would you rather it kicked him in the crotch?'

When Kailash's mother parts the curtains of shells – curious, balking – the two suppress their laughter until Leela rushes to the lavatory hidden behind their house for fear of soiling her sari.

Sometimes, Leela rises from her bed and slips on her pair of sandals. When she chides her to remain indoors, Leela walks out alone. On the dharamsala grounds, the young woman, though uncertain and strained on her legs, shows her own discoveries. Leela, too, is a learned woman – driven to the heart of nature like herself and another loving woman from a different time.

'One need not always wander far to find wonders,' she says. They have walked towards the dwellings of the sweepers and cleaners. She looks over her shoulder, afraid to be caught by Kailash or Subodh, and displeased at herself for the weak morals guiding her suspicions. Leela herself is unbothered. She points towards a pink flower, growing atop a stalk of drooping leaves. The plants stand nestled against the face of a hill, their beds moist with trickling streams that run down the surface of the rocks.

'It looks like every other flower in the valley. But Chagan uses it to treat foot infections in his mules,' she says. Her face is drawn into a serene smile, rid of its tiredness by the fresh breeze and sprays of moisture from the air. She has seen these flowers growing in thick bushes at the edge of the dharamsala grounds. Their proximity making them undesirable and uninteresting. '*Ban kakdi*,' Leela says, a master guiding his charge.

Beetles that rest and feed on animal corpses. Flowers that look like bees. Birds that laugh and mock. Fungus that grows into a worm. Leela walks unhurriedly, careful not to step on blooming flowers or unsuspecting creatures. She regales her hurtling mind with stories of the forest. In the memories of a young child, in Leela's inexhaustible mastery of the world within her reach, the lust for learning prickles with renewed and feverish elation. 'When my child is born, we will all walk together to the forest beyond,' Leela says.

On the days when rains and Leela's bloated feet keep them inside, they lazily sprawl in Leela's room and play cowrie. Though hindered, Leela wins and teases. She sometimes throws the shells onto the *dari* on the floor. It is a show that brings forth a peal of laughter from her. When both tire of their games, Leela tells her of her child. 'My child will grow up happy and content in the valley. And when older, he will spread his wings into the world beyond.'

The world beyond is not a place of joy and contentment, she wishes to intrude, but Leela's smiling face has nestled into her heart. The child is arriving into a world of disappointments, but till he is in the comfort of Leela's devotion, he will be as blissful as she is learning to be.

✿

A peculiar energy runs uninterrupted, uncontrolled in Kailash's house. In the last few days, when his child's entry into the world of aarti and incense becomes imminent, Kailash darts befuddled through the dharamsala grounds. From Leela's village, her grandmother arrives – her frail and hunched figure trudging slowly over the uneven ground. A man, presumably a distant relative of Leela's, holds her hand carefully in his. He whispers close to her ear, guiding her unseeing eyes through the perils of the mountainous terrain.

It is a sight to behold. The entourage spearheaded by the blind woman whose tendrils of grey hair escape the tight bun on her head. A group of younger men and women trail noisily behind her. Pilgrims dash out of their huts to watch the spectacle. Women and children stand at the doors, their heads covered with their saris, a hand carefully placed on the shoulders of their children. It is common knowledge that Leela Ma is in the child's way – her agile temperament only so affected by her condition. Careful of upholding vaguely followed traditions, the pilgrims have been avoiding visiting Kailash's house, where in the front room, she is in the habit of reading palms and charts. Now they wait for her to appear with her new companion.

Sometimes the two rest on benches of stone and wood. She watches the devotees' awaiting gaze on Leela's face, their mouths slightly parted in hopeful anticipation. Leela herself smiles throughout her careful perusal, peering only when absolutely required.

It is a remarkable incident for the pilgrims – this arrival of a woman to bless the dharamsala's child. They gather behind her retinue, whispering among themselves rumours that mould and grow with each row. Consistency remains in only one agreement – it is a sign that their long journey to the doors of God's abode is blessed. Leela is no more than a few days from birthing her son, and the *godhbharai* should have been undertaken much earlier. But the valley is trying. The untimely rains that berate the sheds of the huts and the windows of Kailash's house – soothing the thunderous flow of worries and hopes in the pilgrims on most days – delay the event by several weeks. Leela, however, waits. As composed and content as always.

In the time it takes for Leela's grandmother and relatives to settle into the empty huts of the dharamsala and the house, Kailash himself assembles a strange assortment of equipment. Mostly from the kitchen. Jagdish, Subodh and others trudge in and out of the house, placing their finds onto the table where Kailash keeps his collection of knick-knacks. A transistor, a photograph of his first wife, a bronze candle-holder – its candles dusty and slimy – a chank chipped and broken in several places.

When she has served and fed several of the relatives, she crouches low near the entryway and watches the bizarre flurry of activity. This moment – when the front room buzzes with the unusual noise and clatter of a full house – is the beginning of the last part of her journey. From her vantage point, she is only slightly aware of the shift it marks – a strange departure from the regular that she has come to associate with Leela's abode. Subodh's quiet mien, Jagdish's hurried steps and the unseeing eyes of Leela's grandmother trailing after Kailash's movements with an eerie precision.

A few weeks from now, when she stumbles – panting along the farthest distance into the thick of snuggly rising deodars – she will mark this day as the beginning of an end.

✿

Leela is radiant in her garb of yellow. Her gentle eyes and unmarked skin glow against the brilliance of the colour. Women titter and chatter excitedly around her. In a corner, Leela's grandmother sings, her hands merrily clapping at her knees. A cousin, perhaps less than ten years of age, struggles with a harmonium, her tongue bit between her lips from the strain of concentration, her small hand barely managing to pump at the bellows in time with the flurry of her fingers over the keys.

She is strangely aware of the cacophony that only rises higher with each moment. Before Leela, she would have slyly departed from the occasion, preferring the anonymity of ignored corners and secluded outdoors. But now she watches the women worry over Leela, who leans this way and that to ease the discomfort of her growing child. At the fussing sisters, she only titters. When Leela giggles, covering her face with her swollen hands, the child of sixteen rises to the surface. The sagacity of Leela Ma recedes and in its place emerges the playfulness of a girl. The girl she should be.

She has no fortune or gifts to shower on Leela. No bangles of gold or security to lovingly drop into her lap. The nutcracker, long forgotten in the peti, never crosses her mind. In the many days since Gustav's disappearance from her life – and consequently the end of her visits to the city in the lower slopes of the mountains – she is unaware of the many events that mark the lives of others. Leela becomes her sole marker at the dharamsala, but Leela's domestic life remains a hand's breadth away. From under her bag, she fishes out the carefully curated diary. The flowers have dried and wilted, their moisture absorbed into the pages. The ink has run in most places, and in the spaces where she has drawn their images, the pencil marks are already faded. But their shared love is the only offering she has.

When it is her turn, she gently places the leather-bound notebook in Leela's lap. Perhaps Leela is simply polite – too innocent in her youth to demand more – but her eyes widen at the present. The girl is still turning the pages of her short-lived exploration when she leans down and whispers her blessings into her ear. 'Your child will never live through the horrors of the world.'

✿

The enthusiastic delirium of the occasion trickles down like pleasant winds dying with the peak of day. Their voices get lower and lower until they sit together in corners, softly talking of their troubles and struggles. Leela remains surrounded by distant cousins. Their eyes sometimes seem to sparkle with envy. It has been less than a year since they were combing the hair on their dolls and making mud cakes in summertime. But now she has transcended the playful innocence of their times in their village and become a woman in the embrace of the valley. The womanhood they so desire is hurtling towards them like a dark storm building on the horizon. But the skies are still clear, the breeze still welcome in its caress. In a few months, they will reminisce about their days in the village with nostalgia and dull sorrow.

Kailash and the other men gather chairs and sit around the transistor. Leela's grandmother turns her face towards the commotion, her clouded eyes amused. It is with some effort that Kailash tunes the transistor. On an island far away, men battle for their hard wins. The calm words that float from the speakers are foreign, and the men turn their heads expectantly towards Subodh when the speaker erupts into a piercing crackle from across the universe.

'Venkataraghavan has picked a wicket,' Subodh says. The men erupt in celebration. Kailash grabs Jagdish close into an embrace, and on Subodh's face, she sees a smile that is not suggestive of his otherwise contentious disposition.

Through the spectacle, Leela and her grandmother smile – one of espousal devotion.

'Is Kailash as excited for his child?' she asks. The grandmother regards her carefully. For a moment, she meets her eyes. She seems to peer into her without seeing. Leela, however, is familiar with her bluntness.

'Kailash's concern is more guarded,' Leela says. The gathered women shuffle in their places, awaiting the story they have heard several times before.

'Many years ago, a child was taken from his mother by a beast,' the grandmother says. Her unseeing gaze remains distant, as if she recounts not a myth but her own history. 'The woman was driven to madness, running into the forest, tracking the leopard. She never returned.' She is familiar with these folklores that are garbled until they take mystical forms from the probable incidents they once must have been.

'The men show their anticipation with the vigil they keep in the days leading up to the birth of children in this valley,' the grandmother says.

THIRTEEN

Leela gets only a few years to be a girl before she is christened Leela Ma. The first inklings of it are suspected foremost by her grandmother. She is just a child then, an infant, looking up into her mother's distant eyes. The mother herself is long dead. She remains on earth, alive by all means, but that essence that transcends a simple existence into the plane of truly living, the mother has abandoned years ago. Leela, though, searches her eyes with an innocent intention that only a child can muster. But she is not yet a child. She is swaddled in a woollen cloth – a gift to the mother before Leela was born.

At the age when most infants are unable to focus their gaze, Leela stares into people's eyes as if reading their intentions, their hopes, their most carefully guarded desires. It is discomforting to be laid bare under the scrutiny of one who has not yet developed a truthful perception of the insincere world.

Leela's family is rather large, abounding with distant relatives that spread throughout the plains like the plague. She spends most of her childhood years visited by cousins and uncles and aunts from villages nearby and far away. She grows up with the knowledge that her home is alluring, mystical and seductive, not just to those born in or related to it, but also to those who come into the family through marriage or, sometimes, even long friendships.

In a sea of whitewashed, low-lying homes, the ancestral house is never touched. Black grime and stains of ancient rains mark the original ivory. Save for the narrow barred windows that let in sharp sunlight for a few hours each day in thin slats of colour onto the dusty carpet, the indoors is cold and dark.

Maybe it is the lure of a place that is not completely theirs, or the silent aura of the structure that sings and draws one deep into its heart, that Leela's old and young relatives find it difficult to stay away. Leela – like the child of the forest, like the narrator, like most characters in this story – is an anomaly.

Her birth is not cause for celebration. When she is born, her father confidently raises her clothes, and throwing her back into her mother's arms, runs out of the house, not to be seen for several days after. The gods had long blessed them with sons, but even divine leases expire.

The distant family travels from far away to enquire after the first girl to be born in that ancestral home in nearly seventy years. After all, the greatest of all magics of the ancestral home is its spell that birthed only sons. Those no longer residing in the home themselves father mixed coops far from their roots. Sometimes, men send their wives to the ancestral land in the hopes of siring sons, but it is generally agreed that the child must be conceived under the gaze of the ancestors – and several attempts fail.

Leela's father, the sole inheritor of the ancestral home, does not approve of the upending of his routines either. The elders hurry towards Leela on their first visits. Must the girl look like her mother? Does she have the same bushy eyebrows as all the sons? First, they fawn and coddle, and when Leela stills in her cot to look into their eyes, they turn away, fiddling with their collars and waving their hands around their heads to ward off evil. Leela's aunt, about to mark her with some kohl, places it on her own temples instead.

Children, however, in their rather untainted wisdom of the world, have not yet learnt the various norms and mores, rules and regulations of the faith they are born into. When they see Leela, they see a new child. Perhaps unusual, but still a new child – to be peeped at with wonder and primal joy.

The boys run circles around her, and she moves her head to follow their movements until dizzy. When she cries, her grandmother runs in. A few moments later, it begins again.

The girls are simply satisfied to sit at the edge of the bed and occasionally tickle and caress the infant's supple skin. Sometimes the girls pinch Leela – on her cheek, at her sides, on her small thigh – and though her eyes well up with the sting, she simply smiles and forgives their juvenile misconduct.

✿

Leela grows up in a house of noise and discord. In their small dwelling, she does not expect to see her mother or father for many days at a time. They are avoidant, reclusive, each burdened by their past and present, until neither remembers the child they have borne. In the presence of relatives, their marital affability returns. But once the house has emptied of well-wishers, the racket begins with the dawn of a new day.

In her grandmother's lap, who reads her stories of ghosts and poltergeists, she focuses instead on the sound of screaming and utensils thrown to the floor. For the first few years, her grandmother tells her of a spirit of a young girl that still lingers in the walls. Leela is only fascinated, a possibility that her grandmother considers but forgets in her hurry to dispel questions about the reality.

Leela dreams of meeting Betaal and prepares answers to queries she believes he might ask. The spirit distracts her for some months, but with time, Leela eventually learns the truth. Her grandmother can only hold her close. She holds the child's gaze, apologetic for her home, for the comfort of love and safety that she will never lay in, snuggly.

The child often seeks her mother afterwards, barging into the small room that she prefers over the one where the grandmother and she spend most of their days. She is bruised and bleeding. Leela extends a sympathetic hand, overwhelmed with tenderness she longs to pour into her mother, but is only met with strikes and slaps.

Leela is bothered by her father's actions, though still uncomprehending of their nature. Perhaps that is the predicament of marriages – why so often women cry at their weddings in her grandmother's stories. She does not yet have the words to convey her worries, so she asks instead, 'do you remember what my father was like when he was only your son?'

'He was a good son, Leela Ma,' her grandmother says, 'just like you – full of questions and wonder.' She is burdened by the words Leela chooses and her expectant gaze, waiting for her to answer without needing to put her concerns more plainly.

'His father was a brutal man,' the grandmother says, 'quick with words, even quicker with a whip.' *Perhaps I too am destined to be like this*, Leela thinks, *good now and brutal later.*

The grandmother herself cannot help but worry for the child. Seeds planted in childhood are often difficult to uproot when they grow into poisonous behemoths. The women in her know lean on traditions passed down from the words of the elders to the ears of the young. There is nothing but cruelty that Leela can learn from her parents. But the grandmother has long sensed the empathy of the child, her forgiving kindness and miraculous enlightenment.

After she asks about her father, Leela does not question again. She simply accepts that his soul, like her mother's, and one day her own, is broken. In her grandmother's lap, when she hears the clatter that erupts every evening, she still weeps quietly, and at its end, she simply whispers, 'it is over for today'.

Leela's compassion is unusual, painful to bear witness. Her grandmother worries that she will learn to be too tolerant, unable to tell the difference between the hurting and the evil. In her many decades, she has learnt to tell the two apart, but Leela's heart is yet too large to isolate some and comfort others. When she grows older, she will make it smaller and smaller, till she will love only a few. With reluctance, like her mother.

The grandmother is not learned either. She can only read birth charts and palms. It is a small skill, gradually reaching redundancy, but it is better than nothing, which is all Leela has in the moment. She explains to her the division of the houses, the blessings and sins of each planet, the balance of goodness and evil. The wealth and prosperity of *panaphara*, the groundedness of *kendra*. She holds the child's small palm and traces the lines of her fate – of a long life of joy and comfort. Leela is free of burdening sorrows, and when her grandmother tells her so, she beams with pride at the exuberant life that lies ahead of her.

In the bushes around their home, she tells Leela of medicinal plants. But Leela does not take to the Vedic lessons, nor to the Ayurvedic properties. She remembers the names – kirmani ajwain, sagangur, sugandhbach – but the shape of their leaves and flowers is all she retains in her mind.

'You have a long life, Amma,' Leela tells her grandmother one day. Within the house, the commotion is loud. The grandmother has not heard Leela till now. She is beaming up at her with wonder – it is one of the only two lines she can read, and every evening when the racket rises again, Leela tells her about it. The grandmother is her only companion in this world, and if the mystical sciences say otherwise, to Leela there can be no other way.

'Yes! We will grow old together,' the grandmother says. She tries to smile, but Leela's eyes have already begun to well up. Her father is screaming expletives at his mother, and faintly, the sound of whimpering filters in from the rest.

'Get up, bitch,' the father yells. It is the only thing to be heard now, except the repeated sound of flesh being kicked. These commotions are never one-sided. Though never to raise a hand on her husband, Leela's mother never fails to scream her fury at his actions.

The grandmother carefully lifts Leela off her lap and asks her to remain in the room. Outside, her son is kicking at a broken body. Leela's mother lies unmoving, oblivious to the horror that follows her into death. From behind the door, Leela watches her father kick her dead mother.

✿

Leela sees her father only once again afterwards. The grandmother, finally horrified, grabs Leela's tender hands in her own and leaves the house to stay with her other son. They move to the mountains, where the memories of her mother's hurried funeral are quickly replaced by the verdant scenery. Leela has never been to the mountains before, and the chilly nights and breezy days make her nervous with excitement.

Her uncle is a rich man and manages a tea estate for a richer one. At the edge of the stepped estate, his dwellings are the largest Leela has ever seen outside of newspapers and small magazines. But Leela and her grandmother are given a dilapidated cottage, where their two meals arrive at the same time every day. A man comes early in the morning to bring them hot water for baths and leaves a container of tepid water to drink.

Leela is still only eight years old, and the discrimination is lost on her. Her few hours running around the estate, sniffing at the plants that do not yet smell of tea, are enough to put away the memories of her unbreathing mother and raging father. Her uncle has two girls her own age. They are yet to reach the age when the difference between them and Leela would become a matter of status – when her lack of a second tongue would be an embarrassment, when her shoddy frocks and sandals would be blasphemous, when her talk of charts and lines would be cause for laughter. The three are companions for many years, before a friend from the girls' school asks Leela a question in English, and the status quo sets itself into place.

Her father arrives a year after they have settled into their life in the cottage at the edge of the tea estate. He carries scant jewellery – a few gold earrings, a couple of chains and a heavy ring studded with amethyst – belongings of her mother that she had brought as dowry. The grandmother, perhaps seeing the good son who once plucked flowers for her as a child, pries for some guilt or shame. 'These are her remaining belongings. I burned the rest,' he says, and departs.

At the door, Leela says, 'I forgive you for hurting and killing my mother.' Her father stares at her for long before spitting near her shoe and walking away, never to be seen again.

It is the first time the grandmother raises a hand at Leela. 'It is embarrassing to be so forgiving – to be so docile and gentle,' she tells her.

'Then why do you not take him somewhere? Report him to someone? Make him suffer for what he did?' Leela asks.

Such are the dynamics of the world, the grandmother wishes to say. It would be a bigger shame to tell the world of his actions than to provide justice to an innocent woman.

✿

The fate of the children of others is often of less concern than that of one's own. The education that her sisters receive is unknown, foreign to Leela. The girls will one day become women, queens of their splendorous households, walking behind labouring maids and sweating cooks. In the evenings, women of equal status will gather to grumble about their doddering mothers-in-law who overstay their welcome, and the dawdling and mooching help. They will become aunts who live abroad, dressing their children in scintillating clothes that stand like beacons of their wealth amid the dirty streets of their now-mortifying homes. Their stomachs will roil at the spices and their hands will chafe and peel from repeated washings.

Leela, their companion of childhood, mostly forgotten, will become the greatest shame to their progressive notions. It is their goodwill, their ethics, a testament to their virtuous nature, that their families, in times of tradition, took in a distant relative. It is indignity, then, that Leela makes nothing of herself other than a housewife. Their parents' affections and resources wasted on a child-bride.

Her uncle arrives at their door early one day. It is the first time he has ever done so, preferring to entertain his mother on the lawns of his mansion. Leela is usually expected to stay away from these rare gatherings. An old friend of his, Kailash, has recently lost his wife. 'A freak accident,' he says. Kailash is a good man. A little older and rather unusual, but extraordinarily wealthy. His father was a businessman, cruising through the Independence era untouched and uninterrupted in his dealings with the British – his business dealt in steel.

'Kailash has business inclinations of a different kind,' her uncle says. Leela sits behind her grandmother, on a dari. Her uncle prefers the chair, slightly small for his frame. He fits into it like a hand in a glove, and when he stands a few moments later, the chair rises with him until he shakes it back into place. For now, he continues, 'His brother now runs the business, but he has an ashram in the mountains, on the way to the *dham*. He calls it a dharamsala for some reason,' he laughs.

Her uncle dangles no choice in front of Leela, nor is she consulted on her marriage to a man four times her age. She is sixteen – an unwanted mouth to feed. She is the daughter of a cruel brother – one her uncle prefers to consider not of the same womb. It is not a consultation with his mother either. If it was a question, there would be only one answer.

The wedding is unceremonious. Her grandmother is now bereft of most of her sight, and when she closely examines Leela, she fails to notice that the child wears the same clothes she had worn the day before yesterday. Kailash and his mother arrive in a hired car. In the mountains, he keeps no relics of his wealth in view of the pilgrims, lest they be disappointed by the display so close to the gods. However, he has never sat in anything else, and the prospect of bringing his young bride home in clattering buses makes him apprehensive.

Leela doesn't cry when she leaves. She has no fondness for the cottage where she has spent half her life, nor for her uncle and aunt, nor their young daughters, who do not visit to bid her goodbye. It is the bright leaves of the evergreen camellias, the hordes of cats and kittens that play behind their cottage, her grandmother's hand that held her till it was time for her to be on her own. She kisses her grandmother on the forehead like a mother would before leaving her child for a short while, or a child a beloved pet. 'I will write to you,' the grandmother says. *If only I knew the letters*, she thinks.

✿

Besides her grandmother, she is Leela's first true companion. Her ways are peculiar – often terrifying. Her anxious movements and despondent mind are a cause for worry. But Leela is drawn to the child within her – one whose eyes widen with elation at the smallest wonders of nature, the feverish, almost delirious manner in which she talks of the nutcracker on the fallen oak or the spider she calls Sudarshan in her hut.

In the fifteen months she has been at the dharamsala, there has never been a dearth of people. Women flocked to her like displaced termites to a light bulb. Children, though closer to Leela's age, saw her as not one of their own. But these women never become confidantes, no one to talk to about her dreams for her son, Kamal. Once they see her outward serenity, they cease to see her as a human with worries and desires similar to their own. Leela is not learned in palmistry, nor in telling fates with a glance at birth charts. She simply sees what they ardently wish for and soothes their wandering souls with the words they long to hear. To the pilgrims, she becomes Leela Ma.

She alone demands nothing from Leela. She sees her as a child too young to be concerned with motherhood – a mirror of her own worries that Leela dares not ponder too deeply. Leela has no pity, no sympathy to offer to one who has spent her life extending those to herself. Rather selfishly, Leela needs her easy presence.

✿

By the time it is the hour of Kamal's birth, she and Leela become inseparable. She locks the hut on the other side of the dharamsala and begins anew in a backroom of their house. Sometimes, she falls asleep with a frail arm around Leela's stomach, rising and falling with her breaths – and those of Kamal within her. In the last week, when Leela begins to strain to rise from bed, she declares that there will be no more excursions to the outdoors. It rains often, and the dharamsala grounds are treacherous. The two, sometimes accompanied by Kailash's mother, while away their time playing cowrie, their games growing more complicated with the new and unheard-of rules introduced with every loss.

It is surprising then that when Leela is exerting and sweating in childbirth, she is nowhere to be seen in the room. A midwife fusses and grumbles between her legs. Her mother-in-law stands beside her, ready to scramble at any request from the old woman. Leela had requested – demanded – that she be there when Kamal is born, be the first to hold her child. In the haze, it can be a distant gnawing – a dull ache that hides behind the greater pain of the moment, but will flare again in the dark of night. Leela can only believe that a worry of greater importance had forced her friend to remove herself from the room.

The truth is simpler. She is simply unable to watch Leela's small, childlike body writhe in such agony. With her back to the door, she watches for a while, careful not to tread too close, not to impinge on some unspoken boundary. But Leela, forever a picture of feigned calm, clenches her teeth and refuses to scream. It is no confirmation of her sagacity, rather proof of her youth, this refusal to accept her pain and misery as her own.

She walks past Kailash and into the sleeping premises of the dharamsala. It is late, but a few men stand at the edge of the forest, respectful of the pilgrims' sleeping hours but clanging plates now and then to keep the beasts of their imagination from venturing too close. At the hut, she fumbles for her keys in the pocket of her sweater. Her mind still races with the labour she witnessed earlier, and she briefly forgets that she keeps the keys not on her person, but on the ledge of the window at the back of the hut.

In the dark, she trips, feeling her way along the wall with one hand. She digs near the stem of the bushes and grabs the keys. The sound of rustling leaves fades beneath the throbbing at her temples. When she raises her head, beyond the rhododendrons, in the darkness of the forest, two glowing eyes of green and yellow stare back at her. They blink and, having thus read the situation, turn around.

The leopard has arrived.

FOURTEEN

The alarm she raises travels farther than she imagines in the moment she barges into Kailash's home. She is shell-shocked, devoid of the agency she has long treated as an enemy, even after the beast has blended back into the shadows. Her rude intrusion is met with shushes and silent admonishments – Jagdish's gentle rebuke not to scream, Kailash's widened eyes, and Subodh's leery smile.

'You missed Kamal's birth,' Kailash says, his face softening, relaxing after the strain he believes he has borne equally.

The calm does not last. When she manages to tell them of her sighting – in hurried, strained breaths and broken words – the men rush out of the room, grabbing the utensils they had left on the table in the evening. The cluttered table is a fixture, the dispassionate *haka* as much a performance as an ideation of upholding traditions and beliefs. There is no real fear of beasts at the dharamsala, no sightings close to the establishment. It is a story passed down from mother to mother – a lore as real and as chimeric as the one that washes by thousands each year from distant lands into these mountains. She has broken the illusion, one of keeping this fabled danger safely at bay.

Against a real leopard, the men are incompetent. The dharamsala and its adjoining village are ancient establishments. No tigers or leopards, no beasts other than black bears are ever seen in the region. Closer to the dham in the north, there is a military cantonment. They guard the disputed region beyond, where a route to a valley of flowers is blocked. With so many humans having brandished their marks upon the land, the ecosystem too has bent to the rapacious demands of men.

These weapons of steel plates and spoons, rolling pins and tumblers are mere toys in the face of the marauding beasts of folklore; inadequate against a beast that carries its prey to the hidden crowns of trees. Still, the men keep vigil through the night – their adrenaline and a primitive sense of protection keeping them rooted to the edge of the dark forest.

She too keeps her vigilance at the door of Leela's room, where her exhausted body breathes shallowly. Kamal lies in the crook of her arm. He is small, swaddled into the shape of a watermelon within reams of fabric. He is a crinkled baby, born of many deficiencies, his skin already irritable in the dirty air. Outside, only Leela's grandmother remains, looking out through the windows at the soft pattering rain and the flickering shadows of men in the distance.

When the blind woman turns to look at her, it is with questions. Under her unseeing gaze, she is no longer sure whether she truly saw the leopard or if it was merely a vision conjured by the thunder within her own mind.

✿

It begins with a simple letter. Some *kos* away, a large protected area of the forest is cared for by a retired hunter. She has read about him, in fact, read several books by him – a passionate hunter who became a guilty conservator. Impassioned cries for the preservation of nature ring throughout the country. The prime minister, currently beloved for a few more months, is a known lover of nature. Conservation laws make rounds of courts and assemblies. It is no longer a nation of hunters and killers. The rifles are snatched from the hands of the British and placed into those of local poachers.

Kailash prods her to write the letter. She holds Kamal in her arms, his body light as a feather, as fragile as a cake of mud. Leela recovers in her room, sleeping for most of the day, waking only to feed the child and softly instructing her to care for Kamal till she is well enough to hold him in her own arms for longer. Kailash is hesitant to approach the conservator for the purpose. One of the sweepers has a brother in the army, but when Kailash hails him from his hut by the outcropping, he finds that the younger brother, who had once prematurely alerted him of a landslide, is long dead.

Standing over her shoulder, Kailash dictates the letter.

Respected sir,

I am writing this letter to you with a heavy heart that aches for the safety of his newborn son. I am now in my golden years and since my youthful days, I have dedicated each and every hour of my life to the service of God. At this pilgrim centre, I have seen many things: the elderly wishing for a quick death, young people wishing for better lives, women wishing for better marriages and mothers wishing for happier days for her children. I like to believe that I have done these things with only altruism in my heart, and I have not longed for much in these years.

But in the past few days, since the birth of my son, I believe a dark shadow has cast its spell on my family. My wife, though jovial and young, seems bowed with some worries that she does not share with me. My son, though ruddy-cheeked and chubby, cries his colicky complaints through the night. My mother and I pray every day for better lives for them both, like I have seen pilgrims do before.

In these discomforts, another worry now consumes me. For many decades now, there have been stories of leopards carrying away young children. Once, it so happened that we lost a beautiful young mother to the sorrow of her child carried away. She never returned from the forest, and now I am worried that such a terrible thing has also cast its net on us.

A leopard, large as any you must have seen, was recently spotted at the edge of the dharamsala grounds. It has created a ruckus amongst not just the residents, but even those who stop here on their way to the abode of the gods.

It is our deepest wish that you bring us some relief with your expertise and help us be free of this affliction as soon as possible. There is nothing we are not willing to do to see the end of this leopard which has bothered us for long. I hope this plea of a father would ring home for you.

Please write back to us at the earliest.

Your servant,

Kailash

The letter does not go by post as expected. Instead, Kailash hands it to one of the young boys who care for the mules and asks him to deliver it directly into the hands of the conservator.

'Not with the servants,' he instructs. She offers to send it by mail, but Kailash believes it would be delayed.

'The mail is slow,' he says. 'The boy will be faster.'

✿

The frolicking grounds of the dharamsala become sombre, reclusive. The pilgrims, though not deterred from their path, avoid the open premises as if they too could be snatched away by the leopard. The sky weeps for several hours a day, preparing the forest for the burgeoning assault of monsoon. Several men keep watch at the edge of the forest, more so at night, when beasts move in the shadows undetected and unbothered.

Like his mother, Kamal grows frailer with each passing day. Leela, who lies in fever – severely ignored in favour of the danger that lurks – cannot hold Kamal for more than a few minutes at a time. The tell-tale sound of the curtain of cowrie shells parting at the entrance to her bedroom becomes rare. Kailash paces in the living room but, as if unaware of his wife on one end, turns around just outside her door. When she and Leela's grandmother enter the bedroom, it is in service of the protected newborn. But when Leela produces no more milk, she is left mostly unchecked in her own misery. Subodh is sent into the city to fetch formula. He returns empty-handed.

On days when the skies are clear, she takes Kamal outside. In the sun, his incessant crying fades. Within him, he too carries the love that is shared by her and Leela. Skittish cats draw squeals of amusement from him. Bright butterflies on brighter still flowers bring a flush of joy to his blotched face. She holds him close to her chest, her eyes anchored to the ground with fear of tripping. Sometimes she coos at him, as she has seen Leela's grandmother do so often. Kamal is unresponsive to it, his early cognition too occupied with the new chittering of birds and deceptive meows of kittens.

At night, Kamal sleeps in a crib placed in her room. Leela's fever progresses into a wracking cough. She wakes delirious, refusing to hold Kamal lest she pass her infection to him.

'I will be fine in a few days, but he should not be affected,' she says.

In the crib, Kamal cries and stills. Cries and stills. She sits at the edge of her bed and watches through the night, gently shaking the crib whenever his chest does not rise for too long. She props open the back door that leads towards the outhouse to let in fresh air. Kamal is soothed only briefly in the scent of jasmine and rain.

✿

The boy finally returns. Much later than a mailman would have. The delay becomes a matter of argument between Kailash and Leela's grandmother. For days, they fight, ungrateful words thrown around the front room till Kailash leaves the house in rage. The arrival of the letter calms their hostility. But the letter does not contain news that either of them wishes to hear. That, she knew to be impossible from the moment she had penned the request onto paper. The letter itself becomes a matter of less concern than what follows after.

Dear Kailash,

It saddens me immensely to know that your good family is weighed down with such terrible trepidations. I too have a family of my own and believe that my mind would be bogged with similar worries if such events were to transpire close to my home.

Though my heart cries for your state, I, as a man of the forest, cannot agree to hunt an animal with so few details. As I infer, there has been only one dubious sighting. The valley in which you reside is also home to a bustling village settlement as well as a cantonment further north. It is unlikely that a leopard would wander so close. They are elusive creatures – as fearful of humans as we are of them. Young leopards in their prime are not inclined to create nuisance for people. Injured and senile individuals are more likely to stray close. Even then, such activities might be attributed more to tigers than leopards.

I would recommend observing for a few more weeks around the dharamsala. Keep strict vigilance. There is much activity in your area, and a big cat is likely to keep away. Repeated sightings and paw prints must be present to confirm your suspicions. If I am correct, close to a stream that flows behind the village, there must be several *machans* – old ones from my hunting days. Man them for a few weeks to keep close watch.

If you notice anything out of the ordinary, I will arrive at the quickest. However, since there has been no danger to man yet, I cannot make any promises to cause unfounded harm to the animal.

In your service,

Robert Cavendish

It remains unknown how Kailash's plea to the conservator reaches the ears of newsmen in the heart of the country. Whether it is the servant who was indeed handed the letter instead of the Englishman himself, or the boy, who in search of money, decided to bite the hand that barely fed him. Kailash and Leela, the grandmother and she get only a few days of mourning before the valley is flooded with journalists. They carry small field notebooks, their messenger bags heavy with copies of articles from conservators about indiscriminate hunting and its severe consequences.

'How did you decide that the leopard is a danger if it has never been sighted before this? Why did you think the right course of action was hunting it?'

Subodh herds them back into the city. Some who remain join Kailash's men at night. They are looking for sensation, for pieces that will catapult their careers into greatness. In newspapers, Kailash's face begins to appear again. The picture remains the same as before – shadowed and saturated. But the news that runs with it is no more of his nobility. In richer homes, a familiar tune rings in the news hour, beginning with it the downfall of a pious man.

✿

In the relative quiet of the night, she diligently begins her watch. She keeps the crib rocking as Kamal stills and cries. Stills and cries. From within the house, Leela coughs without interruption. *Did I begin this*, she wonders. Did her mind, broken by the fears within, bring this into the tranquility of this valley? She had seen the glimmering eyes, the very yellow and green that had been written about so often in the memoirs of hunters and naturalists, the yellow and green of Radha's beast. She had seen it recede into the forest, the supple movements of its limbs, just a glimpse of its rosettes lit in the dim light of the crescent moon. She has brought the beast of no one's fears into life.

Sometimes, in Leela's grandmother's eyes, she glimpses suspicion. As if those amaurotic eyes can see the guilt and doubts within her. The old woman traces her movements when she is carrying Kamal around in the front room. From the grounds of the dharamsala, she sees her standing at the door. In her mind, she believes the grandmother is waiting for her to cause harm to Kamal.

She has never fulfilled the needs of others, she realizes. Not her mother, who expected her silence more. Not Kumar, who had put his faith in her to deliver a simple piece of writing. She had failed Mahendra, who was terrified of her actions that endangered his bread and butter. Gustav, who had preferred to steal away like a thief. Leela, who had needed a friend, a companion. A young child who had wanted recognition of her disproportionate expectations – a hand to steady her under the weight she bears.

It is still night when she awakens. The open door has caused the edge of the bed and floor to be pelted with rain. Sheets of it flow from the awning above, curtaining the outside from her view. She rocks the crib again before rising to close the doors. It is rather cold. It must have already seeped into the other rooms, worsening Leela's cough.

Kamal does not cry. She gives a tentative shove to the crib, but Kamal remains unmoving, his eyes focused on the toy dangling over him. When she shoves again, the toy chimes and moves, its rattle lost in the sound of thundering rain. Kamal is still warm, unmoving but maintaining the last of the façade of living. She shakes him quietly, the dread of understanding making her grip around his small arm harder than it needs to be.

The walls of water that she has been keeping at bay now come alive in the corners of her mind. They move closer, grow larger. When she looks up, the sky of blue shimmers and flows. Its weight engulfs her in one single motion, burying her under the terrors she has kept guarded her entire life. She can only draw ragged breaths, quick rising and falling of her chest, though it is not enough. She wheezes, her mind deprived of coherence. In her room, there is nothing that can bring Kamal alive, but she looks around once nonetheless. Perhaps a miracle hides in the corners of the dharamsala, in the house of a man of God.

If it is the cold or the affliction that has been Kamal's companion since his beginning, she cannot answer. In the morning, there will only be statements of conviction. She has killed Kamal. She has killed Kamal while his mother lies ill from his birth and his father fights against the growing appetites for the world's sensationalism. While the dharamsala wards off a fantastical evil.

There is no difference between a dead child and a dead adult, she thinks when she lifts him in her arms. His body is beginning to harden, those pliant traces of flesh that give life already dispersed. He is heavier in death than he was in life. Her feet take her to the broom-shed though she does not wish to be within it. In the bushes of rhododendron, the white bird, still and unmoving, watches her closely – a stranger who interrupts her grooming.

She walks for hours, stepping carefully through the dense foliage, taken by the same fears that had kept her eyes to the ground while showing Kamal the wonders of nature that Leela had shown her earlier. Kamal is dead, but she does not wish to break him further, to leave him with marks of death. She does not think of her apparition that had disappeared into these same depths. She stops at a small deodar, a sapling still. It stands in the shadows of towering others, destined for a short life wanting of sunlight that does not reach to this cruel depth.

It is rather odd, anti-climactic, dissatisfying to bury Kamal under the small deodar. The loamy soil, only slightly affected by the downpour above, gives way with ease under her frantic movements. It still takes a while. Outside the dense canopy, the rain stops and dawn breaks. The sweeper is making his way into the grove of chir on the other side. Subodh, though incensed at the cunning presence of the journalists, awakens early to prepare his esoteric line of questioning. It takes only a moment to place Kamal into the hole, a few more to cover him with the dug-up soil. What took her a lifetime to do is undone in a matter of seconds.

FIFTEEN

In these ebbs and flows of stories, like life, we have forgotten the child slaving to her inquisitiveness. For those observing her – her doting father, her traditional mother, envious siblings and tickled grandparents, the child remains the same, except for the gradually increasing time she spends in the harsh, scorching winds outside. Her mother often grabs her frail arms and threatens to put an end to her adventures if she doesn't confine herself to the cold stone walls of their house. 'The loo will make you sick,' she says, wiping the sweat from her child's brow with the end of her sari.

For those observing her, her frequent excursions are merely propelled by some new knowledge. Like those days when the discovery of distinct formations of clouds had forced her father to pitch a tarp tent in the rains. Or the time when a pair of young shikra, newly arrived in the neighbourhood, was ardently studied with an old, broken and borrowed pair of binoculars. Her mother's worries are logical – the woman is astute, likely to let slide effects that do not threaten the careful web of family image. Her child roaming free for several hours a day is perilous enough, though overlooked for the larger implications it held. A child, however, sickened from heat in the months when mothers were expected to keep their children home, would be a mark of her failings as a mother – the identity she guards closest.

Those observing her for her own sake, rather than for the hopes and dreams of mothers and fathers and grandfathers and grandmothers that they come to embody, would notice that she no longer carries her notebook in her hands. She wakes up late, groggy and irked; turns antagonistic when she refuses to take breakfast at the table where her family of ten sups together. The cooler in her room runs till late, her small body covered with several blankets. She refuses to rise from her fretful slumber; she refuses to return to her room in the evenings. She misses the primate-like morning call of the coucal, feeding on the disturbed life in the freshly watered garden. Several clay pots of water spread through the backyard, the watering holes of stray cats dry.

Her careful examinations and surveys, she forgets as if they belonged to a different lifetime. A skittish partridge carries on in the brambles without her peering eyes, and the group of monkeys, no longer accompanied in their play by a distant cousin, screech in her direction. Outside, she is free from the pleading tone of her uncle. To her young ears, the supplication hurts – a reversal of roles, an adult imploring a child to provide him something. The actions themselves are contradictory, his fingers too large for her frame and his hands entirely unaware of the strength they hold.

She discards the book of whales in a corner after the first time, its bulk and sharp corners reminding her of the inching hand on her thighs. But her uncle arrives every day, in the hours that her mother, accompanied by her grandmother and sister, leaves for the temple in the evening. Her brothers and father carry on a game of badminton in the burnt garden, oblivious to the torment inside the safety of their home. An encyclopaedia of nature, a book of volcanoes, *Pocket Book of Facts*, *Wild Child's Guide to Wildlife*, a comic book, a book of haunted houses – all are relinquished under the bed, where the pile grows larger than the one on her shelf. Her confused silence is pushed and prodded, until one day, her uncle presses the palm of his hand harshly between her legs, digging his fingers into the sharp protrusion of her tailbone.

✿

It always begins the same way – with an enquiry into her latest interest. He is curious, mesmerized by his niece's burgeoning need for complete understanding of the natural world. At the edge of the bed, there is no space for her to move farther. Her fear of what lies ahead leaves her unmoving, her larger fear of consequences keeping her from raising an alarm. It is rather amusing that the child, so loved and cherished, so protected from the terrible events that are the mainstay of several homes, is prematurely aware of the gripping prejudices of the world. She knows of no friend who is neglected or abused at home. Unlike Bablu Nath, she has never witnessed the griping misogyny of men. It is instinct, a coiling sensation in the pit of her stomach, a throbbing pain behind the bridge of her nose that root her in the shadow of her uncle's looming figure.

It is also her uncle's words.

'You are a girl of science, aren't you? Of curiosities?' Sitting beside her, he pleads with her to remove her frock. His eyebrows pull together in desperation, his voice rising higher with every shake of her head. He appears like a child himself, begging his father to buy him a new cricket bat.

'It is completely normal,' he says. He tsks when she says no – her repeated denial grating, infuriating.

'Look, I will show you.' He raises the hem of his kurta and undoes his trousers. A different fear clutches her in that moment. When he thrusts himself towards her small hands, it is that same instinct that makes her comply. If her previous refusal led to this, what would further rejections unfold?

✿

A different kind of curiosity takes hold of her in those summer months. In school, she could have approached a friend, a beloved teacher or even the older girls of the higher classes. She could express her mind's new inability to be still, to remain rooted in the present – it dances between the moments with her uncle and imaginations positioned, never waiting, in the future. There is much comfort in these fantasies of a world beyond, of one not confined within the walls of her room.

In the evenings, her mother implores her to join them in the front room, where a game of rummy begins like a faithful ritual. Her uncle sits beside his brother, his hands previously joined in exchange for her silence – 'this secret remains between us' – now holding a hand of cards. On the narrow diwan, her siblings and grandparents sit huddled together, peering cheerfully into the cards of others. The uncle offers to keep her on his lap.

It is neither curiosity nor that hunger for learning that is now slowly snuffing out like the stub of a relentlessly burning candle, but a deep sense of disturbance that moves her feet into her father's study. Many days – weeks – have passed since the first time her uncle undid his trousers, and this anomalous event unattempted by the others in the family, is beginning to scratch and grate at her. It is painful and disgusting – its normalcy challenged by the diktats of nature that she has observed and memorized.

She simply wishes to know if this is her lot, if its regular occurrence will be intrinsic to her years to come. In their room, she asks her sister about a boy's anatomy, but the sister is still only ten. The children are not growing up in times of liberal thoughts and fabricated awareness. They have been born in the years when certain experiences are best left to the mercies of marriage.

The child should go to her mother, and between painful sobs, explain to her the sudden uncertainty she is feeling. She should place her head into her mother's lap and mourn for the childhood that is being snatched from her. The mother should be aware of the evil that most often lurks beneath the faces of those we know. But the mother herself is encumbered by the weight of several women before her, the women she knows and the women they know. In her youth, her world was one day placed within the borders of a box, deprived of those freedoms that others were granted. One morning, she was just a pig-tailed teenager thwarting the harmless advances of boys in her neighbourhood; the next, she was carrying a child on her shoulders, another in her womb, and preparing meals for several before it was their time to awaken.

She – the child – though uncomprehending, is aware of the pedestal and pressures of her mother's predicament. The length of her skirt, the state of her nails, the leaves and flowers entwined in her hair enrages her mother till she screams and yells at not just her, but all her children, like a sergeant addressing his soldiers. It is painful and undeserved. The mother is guilty, but unless she raises children to one day achieve greatness, there would be nothing that she could say for her long existence. The children are well-mannered, learned and exceptional in ways her nephews and nieces could never be, and when her husband – with a glass of soda in his hand, commanding the ears of his fellow men – tells them of the education he is providing his children, somewhere within herself, she feels a swell of pride that somewhere within, each of them knows it is owed to the mother's effort – unrecognized, uncredited, unthanked.

She approaches her father instead. His choice of roles makes him a nightly visitor – his times of arrival frequently coinciding with the children's departure for slumber. For his rare involvement in child-rearing, he is adored and special. His voice never rises, his words never cut deep; he has never pulled back a hand in the act of slapping before pulling himself together. He brings her books and answers her relentless questions. They are both questioning creatures, and the friend that she could have pulled aside at school also lives in her home. At the age of eight, she is only slowly becoming aware of the unsaid rules of genteel society.

When she asks her father the purpose of a penis, he is aghast. From his chair, a big tome of legal history digging into his trousers, he sees wickedness – the first symptoms of immorality in his daughter. She is much too young to be bothered with such questions, much too shameless. He is distantly aware of the ill-effects of education that can affect the young brains of girls. It is amusing in the early years, but disturbing and unnatural when it is time for her to care for another's home. His older brother has often warned him of it – the men in his university, his tennis club members, even the gardener who works on burnt bushes and struggling grass once every week.

The punishment is delivered by her shrewd mother. Her father hoists her by her arm and carries her into the kitchen. In his burning anger, he can only say, 'Is this what you are teaching her? If I don't pay attention, our daughters will become whores. Do you want to make them like you?' He spits and growls, dribble streaking down his chin and gathering at the corners of his mouth. The child clutches her mother's sari, hiding behind her mother's leg. The mother too stands like an admonished child in the face of her husband's fury. The two, for the moment, are united against his anger in their docility, their submission to their fates. The mother does not need to know what ignites such wrath – if it is some concern for her child or a rational fear of the father. She can only remain still, her hands clutching a *kalchi* close to her chest. It is her sole purpose that is being blemished. When the father, exhausted by his tirade, leaves the kitchen, she can only mete out justice for herself by smacking the child.

✿

This is the child's first brush with betrayal. A sense of doom that stems from the misunderstanding from her parents. Words fail where they had enamoured her for years – their ability to express in themselves all hopes and wonders from before, taking on the garb of a sham. She is detained to her room, the one she shares with her sister, the one where her nightmares tread into reality, the one where her uncle now seeks her out again.

Under her mother's explicit need to uphold certain beliefs of her own, regardless, there is some concern for her young daughter. The mother is not an ignorant woman; she too has suffered horrors that she cannot yet express to her daughters. They are too young, too impressionable; many years of childhood must be allowed until they learn of the evil that will one day lurk in every corner they find themselves in. The mother, however, is naïve, too consumed with the brows that will be raised in her direction and the questions that will be asked only to her – not her husband, not his parents, only her – to truly see what lingers within her own home.

Before she leaves for the temple in the evening, she pulls her brother-in-law aside. 'I hit her today,' she says. 'Will you talk to her?' She is glad that the child, too obsessed with the world of books and nature, has at least one friend who does not walk on four legs. Uncle and niece seem inseparable, hovering around each other like ants around fallen morsels. In these long months of summer, the child has no playmates nearby, and the uncle – long unemployed and struggling to find a footing in the world – and she keep each other from letting interim disappointments become unbearable. Perhaps he could provide the consolation she needs, and by the time the mother returns, the child would have resumed her spirited nature.

It cannot be said anymore if it is neglect or good faith or even preoccupation that has kept the child's parents from seeing what is in front of their eyes. A child previously so vibrant, now stripped of her spark. Often, when she labours over Mahesh's writing or sits beside Mrs Pradhan, even when she watches the nutcracker – unmoving until she is as much a fixture of the forest as the fallen oak or the tree she rests against – even when she is pressing the soil onto Kamal's buried body, she wonders what must have been so paramount in her mother's mind that she could not pull her daughter from the abyss she was falling into.

✿

When her uncle pushes open the door, she knows it is not going to be like other times. There will be no more begging or promises to uphold their secret. There will be no more requests, nor any appeals to her inquisitive nature. Through the thin walls of their home, she can hear the calls of 'howzat' and the dull thunk of a leather ball hitting a bat.

Afterwards, her uncle smacks her across the face. 'You must keep quiet,' he says, his fingers meeting cheekbones where her mother had left the imprint of her fingers. It is surprising how inconsequential it feels to be lying bleeding, suddenly devoid of those flurries of energy that move a body to begin its day or a mind to remain focused on the joys of fluttering leaves or the patterns of the window on the floor during daytime. Her world becomes dull, her vision narrowed. At school, the respite gives her some life, but only enough to enjoy play with the other girls; at home, she remains in bed, avoiding the flesh of her sister, the feel of which serves as a traumatic reminder.

A year later, however, her uncle leaves – the job in the mills never realized. Her father arranges for an apprenticeship at a lentil factory, and one day, she awakens to find that he will no longer appear at her door nor press his hand into her face until she struggled to breathe. Years later, at her brothers' weddings, they will meet – he will ask after her performance at school and be surprised that the brilliant child had become one of the several who never amounted to much; had become like him. Her mother would bring out pictures of the two. 'They were inseparable,' she would say, pointing at two figures reclining on a diwan – her face drawn with moist eyes and him smiling brightly in the background.

The day before she leaves for college, she stands at the threshold of the kitchen. In these ten years, her mother has aged – once beautiful in her colourful sari, now refusing to get out of her nightdress throughout the day. Her face is wrinkled, skin gathering under her chin that stands out like a wooden doll. She is the last child in their home – the brothers working in faraway cities, and her sister married, with a child of her own.

In a *tandoor*, her mother places dough for baati, the child's favourite. It is a parting meal, and instead of nurturing words, there is only food. What she has come to say, she has chosen to keep unsaid for many years, the first doubts of it arising in her soon after her uncle leaves. It is the time when her mother stops wearing lipstick in the morning or combing her hair before going out in the chill of the morning with a container for milk. Many years have passed since, and the mother and daughter have picked bones of a different kind, but the end of her life in this home would be unfinished if not for this exchange.

'Did you know what was happening?' she asks. Her mother does not move, does not look over her shoulder. The question has been long overdue. She lifts the lid of the tandoor and turns over the baati inside – one careful flick of her wrist after another. Through the hole in the bottom, she stokes the coal with a stick.

'When you are a mother yourself, you will learn that your family is your life's work,' she says. 'It would have been a great shame to me if others had learned of it.'

PART 3

THE LEOPARD

SIXTEEN

The mahouts and their elephants are the first to leave. The news of impending disaster reaches them through their inquisitive mouths and ears, the danger both exaggerated and subdued along the way. The mahout hears it from a timber feller waiting in line to collect his day's wages, his brow beading with sweat long after he has put his mechanical axe down, who hears it from a khadi-clad man employed to manage those who speak his tongue, who hears it from the supervisor watching over the logistics of sheesham logs, who himself hears it from the managers who often partake in glasses of jhol with workers who perform night duties at the gates of the hydraulic power plant.

The village itself is not aware of the powers that build behemoths over rivers, changing the course of nature; the beast that is rarely restrained by the demands of man. The rains, though late in their arrival, unleash furious downpours until the ground clogs, unbreathing and drowning. Children make games of it in the first few days of monsoon, their boats of paper propelled by winds that later thrash the rain in wayward directions. Some jump into puddles, dirtying the hems of their frocks and knickers until their mothers take a stick and beat the frivolity out of them. The elders too are relieved, though their ways are different. 'Back in our days, it would rain from Jyeshta to Magha,' they tell the uninterested children, their eyes fixed on the drizzle pattering comfortably.

But this is not the village of their childhood, those days and this day are separated by several decades in which the forest has been denuded to the horizon; the previously unfamiliar expanse now bare and bright in their sight, the foreground covered in ringed stumps. A hydraulic power plant, with its promises of jobs that pay in paper money rather than stingily doled-out coins and favours, brings in men in ties and noises of metal and construction that fade out the sounds of the forest, the sounds of their childhood. The military outpost arrives soon after in response to claims over the river, its water neither theirs nor of a separate nation's, though both cry over it. These troubles are, however, much in the future, not yet escalated to national concerns, when the sounds of machines whirring into the night are further drowned by those of bullets, when this very village that now scurries about under the thundering rain will be evacuated, several homes uprooted, several children growing up with worries they have no names for.

A farmer brings this news to his wife. 'The mahouts say the river is overflowing,' he informs her over a late meal. He has been consulting with the elders well into the night. Man's machinations have brought many troubles over these past decades. Landslides destroy several homes or wash away paths that connect them to the other villages, forgotten homes of wives and mothers. One summer, the rice grows, filling the village's granaries and bringing in capital; the next season it floods; next it dries. The power plant men buy land from farmers, who struggle to buy more land from the power plant men in other areas. The river dries where it earlier flowed, its direction changed with the dam. Upstream, where the village resides, they can see the hindering bulk of the dam, the river that had previously dried now slowly swelling.

'The dam keeps it away,' she replies. She is of a simple mind, he thinks, so easily swayed by what she hears from other women. He, too, is only faintly aware of what occurs on the other side of the dam. He has stood at its edge and seen the river of his childhood contained within its borders. 'It's a miracle, it is,' one of the men in black suits says to the gathered group when the village is first invited to see the new wonder. Now the mahouts, the very ones who had helped in the building of this dam, have departed for distant hills with their elephants. The shed is emptied, devoid of all except the faint smell of musty hide, dung and hay.

It is no surprise that the happenings are kept from the villages, both upstream and downstream. The villages are still powered by kerosene lamps and coal-filled kangris. The reservoir is not for them, and when a mahout brings in the news that the power plant itself is emptying quickly, there is no other possibility than a malfunctioning dam. 'It's going to break,' he says. 'We shouldn't have allowed her to stay here. Our reserves are scarce and we don't know how long a woman like this will mooch off us.' He throws his plate in his wife's direction – towards her feet, not her face, where it would leave marks. Behind a flimsy wall, she lies exhausted, unaware of the discord she has brought.

Her arrival in this village coincides with that of the climbers. The colour of their skins and the bulk of their forms draw the eyes of children who have not lived in the era when men like these were mainstays in the covers of the forest. Some miles to the south there is a mansion, once lived in by an avid ornithologist who would sometimes foray into their village. He wanted to know the names of his beloved birds in the local tongue. Now the mansion has stood empty for several years, the ornithologist returned to his native land of sparse birds.

Her arrival, however, takes precedence over that of the climbers, who quickly plead for some time in the warm houses, their tents inefficient in the heavy rains. She is alone, profoundly purposeless. To the farmer's wife, she spins a story of a sister in a distant village. 'I have lost my way,' she says, but when asked the name of the place, she, unfamiliar with the region, is unable to lie further. It is suspicious. The village is rife with stories of haunted spirits, and the elders, though pious, are rather disinclined to believe them. The children's imaginations flow unbridled.

The whispers of the disaster bring people out of their homes, who scurry about the grounds with panic masked as intention. An old man wanders about knocking on people's doors. In the sheets of water gathered on stone and soil, he slips briefly before uprighting himself against a pillar. The farmer's wife has provided her with a quilt to lie on and a bowl of dal and rice left over from the afternoon meal. It has been no more than a few days since she began her journey into the forest, but she is already haggard, the last remnants of her previously manageable life giving way to taut, sickly skin. When she hears the commotion in the early hours of the morning, she too leaves the house to join the hubbub. The rain, though subsided, has left the village muddied. The rumbling clouds shake the earth every few minutes, and the village lies in a sombre shade.

The villagers gather around the climbers, twelve in total, though the six white men command much more attention and respect than the sherpas who guide them on their quests. The sherpas stay at a distance, part of neither the climbers' advices nor the villagers' hopes. The climbers' words are, however, lost in the ether that absorbs one language and delivers it in another. They gesticulate profusely, pointing towards the distant peak that is their destination. The villagers watch dumbfounded. The elders lean closer to the climbers as if it is simply the state of their senile ears that keeps them from understanding. In return, the man who flails his hands the most yells his responses louder.

She goes to stand by the climbers, who give her only a perfunctory glance. Their purpose here seems larger than the threat that scares the village. From a few words here and there, she understands that they are asking for a way further into the valley. The loudest man has been to these mountains before. He smiles briefly, nostalgic for his youthful adventures. But that route is now closed, the trek overrun with unmanageable growth. The other way is susceptible to landslides, and in the rains that have battered the area over the last twenty days, they are afraid that some disaster, similar to the one they are unbothered by, would affect their journey in horrendous ways.

This is the story she puts together. Of the little she understands, she latches onto the name of the valley – her destination. The destination of the beast. She feels the beast's presence as if it is an extension of herself. It takes cover under thick canopies, the downpour only lightly pattering on its black and orange coat. It is not ideal shelter, exposed and injured as the beast is. It should have climbed a tree, rested on a strong branch. But of a paw, only a part remains. The flesh itches and throbs until it feels the pain behind its tired eyes. When it licks it for comfort, a rancid taste spreads through its mouth. Much like her, it too is aware of a presence following it into the forest to finish what was started in another valley further south. The fear becomes vigilance until it is unable to rest, its eyes honed into the thicks where it came from.

Though concerned for the village's fate, the gathering never lasts more than a few minutes at a time. The rains begin again, the people waiting at the threshold of their homes for the moment when they could counsel once more. But the time never arises again for the day, and the village retires for the night. The thunderstorm picks up at night, swaying even the sturdiest trees with an eerie noise that keeps the children awake and the mothers worrying over their health.

She too lies with her eyes open at night. She dreams of the beast, feels its fear and pain. It is bothersome – unusual – when its chest rumbles with a helpless groan. When she wakes, she hears whispers. The farmer and his wife talk in a quiet hush. It is their concern for the truth behind what goes on near the dam. The power plant is abandoned, the village only learning of it when some men go to enquire after the rumours. Even if the rumours are unfounded, the awaited rain has ruined crops of potatoes and cabbage, leaving several in the village without a livelihood for a part of the year. A cliff towards the southern edge of the village crumbled like a mound of flour the day before. The area itself is uninhabited, but the entire village is on a hill hugging the last vestiges of the river contained within the dam.

'She has brought ill tidings with her,' she hears the man say. In the ensuing pause, she listens to the ragged, panicked breathing of his wife. 'We do not turn away those in need,' she says. From her place, she hears the rustling of sheets and imagines that the wife – perhaps bothered by her husband's accusations – has turned her back to him.

In the morning, it is decided that the climbers will travel to the military establishment in the north. When the men, in the hours when the rain subsides to a drizzle, travel towards the dam to stand at its edge, they see a river overflowing, reaching its menacing fingers towards the ledge. With the plant abandoned, the floodgates remain closed. The peril – till now a rumour – becomes a commination.

The climbers are inspired into action by their own needs, convey the sherpas. The expedition has been a few years in the making – a soft battle raging between nations to climb the peak first. The sherpas barely understand the climbers themselves, only one is slightly learned in their language – enough to guide them towards and up the mountain. They are sons of former sherpas, and in the time between the loud man's first foray to a different mountain and this, the knowledge of the language is lost.

The village waits for the return of the climbers. It is a short journey upstream of the overflowing reservoir. The people move in and out of their homes with the rain. During the short gatherings, the sherpas tell them of the climbers. 'Stubborn men,' they say, 'come to conquer the holy mountain.' Through the thick cover of trees, she glances at the peak in the distance – its shoulders, which will give way to the glacier, still a massive stretch away. It is madness, she thinks, to choose of one's own accord such trials. How simple must one's life be to allow for the seeking of such thrills. To the villagers, her stories of a lost sister – a little weak in the mind – are of a similar madness. In the rising panic, she, however, becomes a part of the people. She sits with the elders, her words unheard. She believes they should have moved upstream by now, perhaps before they had learnt of the abandoned plant. It is not too late, she says, when the cold evening unleashes the rain once again. Her destination too lies in that direction, but in the days in which she has been in the village, the cries of worried children who are confined to the mundanity of their homes, and the women – deprived of knowledge that men guard as if its conveyance would unsettle the balance they have created for centuries – walk from one home to another to say and hear the same few snippets they hear from others.

The climbers return the next morning. They are accompanied by men in uniform. With half the village in tow, they walk to the dam to confirm what the villagers have reported. It is not enough to simply believe it – they must see it with their own eyes. A couple of climbers stay back in the village. An establishment upstream is flooded – water up to knees and people's belongings floating away in the river. 'The people have been swimming in it to retrieve their lives,' a sherpa translates. The climbers' equipment is expensive and necessary, and while they wait for the return of their companions, they move away from the villagers to reflect among themselves on their next steps. The sherpas, once again, are left out of the decisions.

✿

For the next two days, the thunderstorm picks up until the sounds of it become so commonplace that even children stop being bothered. At the farmer's house, she becomes restless. The husband and wife talk late into the night, repeating the same information they have been since she arrived in the village, and sometimes lowering their voices to whisper about her and her untimely presence. At times, she is tempted to crawl over to the other side of the room. She would shake the blanket at their feet and explain that she too was hindered in her undertaking. She too had once lost a home and feared the arriving days. But when these whispers travel across the thin wall, she is plagued by the beast whose whimpers she hears louder with every passing day.

In these rains, when no spot remains dry and comfortable, it suffers the furies of nature. The wound that was supposed to dry and heal now festers. The flesh discolours to yellow, then green and finally a stinking brown – and where the claws had dug into it, now tatters like the end of a hurriedly torn cloth. Its shelter is never agreeable. The rain patters on its coat throughout the day, seeping into its bones like an unyielding parasite. When the skies clear, it strains to its feet and travels a little distance before collapsing near an acceptable protection in wait of the next moment.

The village itself embodies the pained restlessness of the beast. Life and time are measured by drizzles and downpours. Waiters and watchers run out of their homes at the first sign of relenting skies but fail to come to conclusions. There is no more doubt in the village that the dam is now a threat – if not immediate, then imminent. The climbers too are bound to the fate of the village. The trek to the mountain is likely to be flooded by the breaking of the dam. She senses that they would have preferred to leave earlier, or perhaps arrived earlier, when the power plant was still occupied and the villagers were only slightly concerned by the unrelenting rains. Among themselves, they chide each other for thinking of what could have been, much like she relishes in her imagination of the same.

The men in uniform, after showing the climbers back to the village, leave. They promise prompt assistance – vehicles or horses to help the village move farther north, where some of the other villages have been evacuated. It gives hope to the villagers for a few days. They stop huddling around in the cold winds and conversing in circles. But no help comes for several days. The coal and firewood seep with moisture, hearths cold and unmanageable. They cry at the unfairness of it all – mothers weeping at the breasts of their children who sicken from the lack of sun and sniffles. Once again, they have been forgotten in the grand machinations of the nation.

It is decided that people's belongings – mostly grains and small fortunes – would be moved into the abandoned elephant shed. It is situated on the upper reaches of the hill, hopefully farther from the impending damage. A man in a battered sweater and *topi* moves from door to door to assemble only the needful. 'Once we have moved the belongings, we too will move,' he says. The climbers are strong and empty their own bags to help carry the load of the village. The farmer's wife hands her heavy blankets and some covers to bring with her. The path to the shed is steep and slippery. The air, pregnant with dew, quickly settles on the blankets, bending her knees and leaving her panting. It is not a long journey, and for the first few minutes of it, she tries to catch up with the climbers. To one of the sherpas, she relays the same story of a lost sister. He carries two bags – one on the front and another on his back – and she suspects that he has not heard the plea in her words. 'The valley you will need to pass through is where I need to go too,' she says. To her request of conveying this to his other companions, he just nods.

She waits for him to talk – to perhaps refuse curtly or shoo her away with some hurtful words. But he does not seem a man of many words, and soon the time passes for further discussion. The rain too begins again – one moment just a few drops on cheeks and a sheet of water the next. Several people slip on their way to the shed, whose eaves and roof are now visible. By the time she reaches the large tin doors of it, the blankets are dripping, devoid of their purpose.

It is in the nature of dreadful frights to come alive in the dead of night. Long after she has been awakened several times by those apparitions of the beast that equally confound and trouble her; long after the farmers have stopped whispering and fallen into a tired sleep after moving their belongings into the cover of the shed; long after the sounds of the storm fail to disturb, rumblings begin to shake the village.

She is fighting a battle of wills with herself, forcing her eyes that fall closed of their own accord to remain open. The beast sprawls on its side, its paws stretched out towards the trunk of kumkum. It first tries to rest its head on its paw, avoiding pressing the injured one under the weight of its head. The paw stops throbbing and it falls into a fitful sleep – one brought on by days of atrocious labour. The other legs now ache from having to carry the weight of the dead, and in its sleep, it dreams of a woman chasing it into the forest. She stalks closer – no further than a few kos from where it rests. She too is slowed by the onslaught of rain, but it walks slower, needing to stop more often, and before long, in its dream, she catches up. It is a mercy, it believes, but when she steps closer, the beast awakens with a sharp pain. Its head drops onto the rotting flesh and the exposed nerves burn in searing agony.

The beast's helplessness is not hers to bear, but the dreams make her timorous – doubtful of this task she has undertaken. Her reverie breaks with the first faint rumblings. *It is the clouds*, she thinks. Soon there will be a thunderclap, and though the sounds will drown in those of the storm, children too will wake from their sleep and cry in fear of what they do not understand. The bowels of the earth move again. She feels the reverberations under the floor where she rests. She places her hands on the cold floor outside her quilt and with widened eyes, tries to adjust to the darkness as if seeing would reveal what crawls under the surface.

There are no shrieks from within homes, no alarm raised by wakeful villagers to abandon their sleep and run towards the hill of the elephant shed. She has barely risen from her quilt to join the farmer and his wife, who she imagines have also been harangued by the new sounds, when the anticipated thunderclap momentarily sends blinding light through boarded windows and gaps in the walls. From around the wall that separates the granary where she sleeps and the one room that comprises the dwellings of the farmer, she has only spotted the wife putting her palm on the floor to rise, when the earth begins to groan and shake as if angered, and the wall of the house collapses under a wave of water that pushes all three further into the granary.

The events of the next hour come to her in snippets – the bursting panic shared throughout the village like a thread connecting them in their horrors leaves her with very little beside immediacy. The farmer's wife, discerning in her support to her whose arrival the husband had likened to bad omen, is crushed under the debris that breaks the wall of the house. She catches it in the corner of her eyes, uncomprehending except for the waves that crash into her chest, and it isn't until much later, when they can move about in the water, that the farmer finds his wife – her hand reaching out from under the surface, her entire body mangled under a massive chunk of cement from the dam. Outside, the water is more dangerous – debris catches people unawares and most cling to fallen walls and roofs, waiting for the current to subside. She watches a child only barely able to cling to an eave, get washed away by the muddy flood. A woman's head struggling to surface finally stops thrashing. The farmer joins her outside, his forehead creased with concern that he can yet voice, and his eyes moving feverishly in search of his wife.

In the distance, the hill of the elephant shed – where the village, the climbers and their guide decide to stay in fear of their own equipment that might rust and die faster than they should; where the village had decided to move right at dawn, no more than a couple of hours from this moment; where the mahouts, more astute in their quick decision, had unchained their elephants and left – appears to ripple like a mirage in a sandy desert. The rain continues to thunder down and the river, overflowing with its freed water and debris from the dam, churns furiously below. It is rather comical, she thinks – soundless and distant – when the hill, finally devoid of several layers of its surface, collapses into the river below.

SEVENTEEN

Not much of the village remains after the river slows – neither the structure nor the people. Where the water previously filled houses to the brim, drowning children and non-swimmers, it now recedes until the village can be traversed on foot, wading through it. It was not a large establishment. Paved roads, though potholed and perhaps neglected for several decades, connected clusters of homes. Trucks carrying packaged goods, a rage in the cities, drove in every week, and a man who magically arranged the front of his house into a shop, sold packets of snacks at marked-up prices.

The largest house, set further apart from the cluster, belonged to an orchard owner. He himself rarely went to the farm, his managers and minions overseeing its functions and activities. But he kept the lawns and fences of his home as protected from the villagers as if his newfound prosperity now set him apart from the people he once played marbles with. Every evening at the village centre, people gathered around a bonfire. Some men huddled at a distance from the fire, where its light left an illuminated spot on the road, but far away from where the general revelry of the village gathered closer to wrap up the day. Their games of marbles, now involving money carelessly thrown on the road, were ignored. The village had entered an era of modernity, and for the hundred or so houses that made it, would soon be mired in those dreams of materials that can neither be sustained nor disregarded.

Now there are only figments of their lives. Most would move far away, where the cost of resettling is lesser than that of rebuilding their homes, where the memories of their lost ones retrieved from under debris – most left under the large stones – and burned in a pile on water-clogged earth would haunt them for a lifetime; where their children would suffer for the lack of affection from their parents, and so on. Someone far away, in a vest and kurta, would slap a number on the losses and send his thoughts and prayers. Addresses of other villages and even towns and collection numbers for petty money would summarize their lives. Years would pass moving from window to window of government offices, seeking reimbursement for most of their existence.

In the retreating sea, she is parched, shaking with hunger and shock. The farmer, in the hope of finding his wife, had left earlier. The current then was much faster. He had jumped, and in the blink of an eye, his body had been swept away. Catching the branch of a fallen bael, he had steadied himself before letting another current wash him further.

The river below reveals land. The drop, though dangerous, has settled. Debris from the dam, trees and the occasional pan left behind as non-essential float lazily on the surface. Her muscles have locked themselves into the grip of a python. It is the fear of the bodies now floating past – a severed hand, a thigh bumping into a desk, a head, pale and macabre from the exsanguinated body. The bodies, their open eyes turned towards heaven – now clearing as if mourning and recognizing the pressing needs of the village – pass peacefully northwards. It is an eerie sight from her perch, her cold fingers curled stiffly around a rebar.

Showing uncharacteristic faith, she jumps.

The village rises as if from slumber. The morning arrives unbothered. Drenched birds angrily shake the rain from their feathers and announce their disapproval. The sun reflects off dew on fallen branches. A rainbow forms in the north. Only the villagers are truly affected. They gingerly step out from behind razed structures, some from within the homes where they had found shelter. Others appear at the edge of the forest beyond, from over hills and cliffs. The slow trickle towards the centre is mundane, regular. As if it is a common morning and the people have gathered to fill containers from the tap that is left running throughout the year, lest it freeze.

Their steps, however, are demonic – unhurried and hindered in the river that reaches up to their chests in places. Their eyes are haunted, flitting furiously and searching for a lost child, a mother, a husband who could have held them in the moments after the flood.

The time is not yet ripe for wails and shrieks of grief and horror. Under the water, several bodies are trapped, and it will be some more time before they rise to the surface, the flesh already softening from the water's harsh touch. The people mill about, some in unspeaking groups and some moving away from them as if the gathering signifies an event they are not yet ready to face. She wades away too. Far from the centre, where men now dive into the murky water to see what is left of their lives.

Objects of fragile domesticity float around houses. Most of the walls have fallen, and people use the larger openings rather than doors. Inside one, a woman lets out a heart-piercing cry. She waits – with some others – far from the door, afraid that her sorrow and misfortune might touch them too. The woman appears, her shape revealing itself gradually. In her arms, she carries a young girl, part of her skull shaved off near the temple. The blood is washed away, and the pink matter of her brain glints in the sun. The woman stumbles near the door, and the child drops into the water. For a while, no one moves. Perhaps it is a better death – to forget the girl in the river where her mother cannot mourn the completeness of her being, where the memory of her disfigurement, being so short, might one day drown, leaving only images of a time before the flood.

✿

It rains only softly after that Monday. The news is slow and novel, and except for a few lines in a local newspaper and a small column hidden between sensation in larger ones, the destruction unleashed by the dam upon the village is never heard of. It takes a few decades, the arrival of a new generation – one with perhaps more empathy – to bring the forgotten village to justice. Monies are given to children – now elderly – who had lost families, livelihoods and that same will she did long ago.

The dam, however, becomes a matter of much discourse. Was it the heedlessness of the government or the neglect of those who abandoned it without warning? In the time it takes for the water to recede and for hordes of men to arrive to salvage what remains of the dam, the village is emptied.

That first night, no one sleeps. On the roofs of lost homes and branches of trees, previously inaccessible, people remain stunned, unmoving. Throughout the morning, the water retreats – like those unusual arrangements made for an overstaying guest, hastily undone to reintroduce the family routine. Some people decide to walk, propelled by an unspoken and unmade decision to simply get away. She too walks aimlessly, a little apart from them, towards the hill of the elephant shed. Her only possessions are the clothes on her person and the presence of the beast.

Since she woke to the sound of the dam giving away, she has not sensed it either. The beast gives her this mercy. It tends to itself for a while as she wanders through the ravaged village. It is much farther now, her exile here having put a distance between them that will take several days to cross. But it is a relief that the beast is far from the terrors of this village. It will not drown or be washed from a promontory. It will not be buried under mud and rocks or crushed beneath the remains of the dam. It will remain, waiting for her until she finds her way to it.

On the hill, she hopes to run into the climbers. The landslide that took the hill has left the river even dirtier. Closer up, she sees hay floating on the surface. On the muddy trek, her legs sink several inches, though with the hill now denuded, the chance of another landslide is so low that she walks with a confidence she has not felt in many years. There is some faith in those dogged eyes of the loud climber that convinces her that the group survives. Like those who had abandoned the power plant, they must have sensed the disaster waiting to happen – perhaps the same loud rumbling she had heard.

She does not have to walk far before she sees them sliding down the hill's slope. The loud climber and the sherpa – their inadequate translator – hurry along in front. The others soon appear from above, first the climbers, then the sherpas. At the very back, a climber walks slowly, his bulk supported by another. He limps, his face drawn in pain, and for a moment, she believes she can hear his groans of agony, like those of the beast.

The climbers in front pass her without much ado. The sherpa asks if there are many survivors but does not respond when she asks after their state. Her hope hardens into suspicion. She could wait for the limping man – but it is the climber in front, his eyes wide with urgency, who draws her feet back towards the village.

✿

She sleeps as if complete surrender to unconsciousness would bring back the flood. On a mound, damp and soggy from the water but drier than the village grounds, the remaining people gather. At some distance, surrounded by brambles and under the cover of a small grove of rhododendrons, the climbers too spread out their few belongings. The loud climber – Edwin, his name, as she finds out – deposits his injured friend with the other climbers and begins his journey towards the hill. From the mound, the villagers watch the hurried activities of the men. The figures from this distance hide behind her thumb, but Edwin's haphazard movements in the rabble of the shed are unmistakable. His urgency, perhaps at the cost of all else, belongs singularly to his desire to climb the mountain. When the climbers leave, unwary of the injured one, the sherpas whisper among themselves.

'He is mad,' one says. 'How will they climb with barely any equipment left?'

'And what of the limping man?'

His swollen ankle rests on a bed of jackets and wet, folded blankets. The man has a narrow face and a high, sloping forehead – in some distant science, a sign of great intellect. But he is rendered unmoving for most of the day, whimpering in his sleep. To the west, the village spreads out, desolate and destroyed. Some still swim in the waste, hoping to find their loved ones or loved things. On the mound, women cry in corners and men gaze into the distance with expressions so blank she fears life might leave them – though it had not, only a few hours ago. Most, tired and despairing, bide their time for the river to recede – and for their families to reveal themselves.

Edwin's mulish treks and digging provide moments of relief. Their vacillation – or simply the impossibility of forecast – is briefly soothed by the frowns and lines of fixation on Edwin's face as he carries, first, a pair of steel crampons and a drenched tent, and next, a bag full of peeling notebooks caked with mud. His movements become the rhythm to which she drifts in and out of sleep – the slow, probing walk marking a few minutes of peace, and the sudden, frenzied ones a signal to awaken and watch the mad climber.

In those few seconds, she is unable to ignore the beast. As if fearful of the village's fate, the presence recedes. In sparse glimpses – as rare as villagers finding their families on the mound – she sees it walking lazily, dazed and muddled, towards a valley. She commits the images to memory: tall, towering brown oaks; a lone horse chestnut, growing lonely among the rianj under which it rests briefly. Further ahead, the sounds of a burbling river beckon. It is thirsty – those small, drawling sips from a stream of rainwater long forgotten. On its injured leg, it struggles to lower itself to take a hearty drink. Wary of rustling bushes, it scampers away. The river is not far now, and in its clear expanse, it can lie and drink.

Edwin's frequent treks to the hill are soon taken on by the villagers. Perhaps inspired by the collection of retrieved equipment he manages to bring back, they too follow after the climbers in search of lost belongings. The mound cries with hunger and grief, and for those assured of their lost families, the hill becomes the final hope. Edwin sometimes shoos them away when each journey sees more people following. He is a reluctant leader to the villagers, though one of dictatorial authority to the other climbers. These are not his people, nor does their presence serve the larger purpose that drives his feet from the mound to the hill. From the mound to the hill. From the mound to the hill.

His stomach grumbles with the same rebellion as that of the villagers now following him. Before long, the people will return to their senses and begin a slow march to the military camp, where there would be food and shelter. Silently, he blames the village – and the rare spark of benevolence he felt in those moments when he chose to stay and help – for the predicament he now finds himself in. *The French team would never have done something like this*, he thinks. His equipment is either lost or waterlogged. The rains have slowed and the path is perhaps clearer. It is the optimum time to cover the forested valley beyond the military camp. A short brown man walks beside him, and in his frustration, he pushes him slightly – a rather gentle plea to be left alone when all he wishes is to burn the remaining village down.

✿

All things pass. Even grief. Especially grief. A child forgets the face of her young mother. A young mother forgets the feel of a lost child on her breast. Mrs Pradhan forgets those lonely years with her unloving husband. Kumar forgets the torment of neglect. Bablu Nath forgets the adoring gazes of his parents. The child of seven forgets Bablu Nath. The child of nine forgets her uncle. The villagers will eventually forget the tragedy that has struck them – and one day, the slope of a wife's nose and the scratchy feel of a lover's beard. They will forget certain corners of their destroyed homes and the feel of an old rug. And it begins on the mound.

Three men gather in the morning to discuss the best route to the military camp. The women and children are hungry, they say, as if their own hunger is somehow less urgent. They whisper to the sherpas, asking them to employ the help of the climbers. Certain colours carry more weight. The camp, which had previously failed to provide the promised assistance, might be inclined to act if they knew of the injured climber. He is beginning to awaken, sometimes asking to be left alone so he can turn on his side and relieve himself. The swelling remains, but miraculously, without food or movement, his mind returns.

On one shoulder of the mound, the village collects their loved ones. In the moist heat of the ceased thunderstorm, the stench is unbearable. Though several times a day, a grieving person is drawn to the morgue, people soon shift their camps farther from it. Edwin grumbles when the request is made. The climbers stand behind him, straining their necks forward to parse the emotions of their friend.

'I cannot delay any longer,' he says. Words the translator need not explain. It is evident from the exasperated waves of his hands and the roll of his eyes. Perhaps the villagers forget the same two legs that carry them. Perhaps the burden of what has come to be weighs them down so heavily that they now need the assistance of these reluctant climbers. The men fold their hands and beseech the group to approach the military camp. Edwin remains quiet through their pleas, his eyes unreadable, devoid of expression. Watching from the back, she thinks this is her opportunity.

That night, she sleeps peacefully. In her dreams, the beast collapses in bushes of blue poppy with exhaustion. The sky is clear, and under the stars, it raises its paws into the air and stretches on its back. Its limbs lengthen, its spine pulled taut, and for a moment, relief floods through its once-nimble body. The pain of the lost limb is briefly forgotten – until extended so in the air, it throbs with a vengeance, and the beast falls once again onto its side.

EIGHTEEN

Edwin is the last person to shape our – and her – memories of this story. He is born to an Englishman and an Indian woman. His father, he believes, is a good man. Though he never mentions the Indian woman, he is kept in the family alongside Edward, the son born to his father and Lady Harris. Edwin, in the simplest of words, is a bastard, but he is never made to feel so. Except for the few times when Edward, a few years senior to him at school in England, tells his friends about it, who tell Edwin's classmates and so on, until the news spreads like wildfire to be dissected and prodded with malice and scrutiny. Edwin, however, learns that news, like all things of a certain scandalous nature, is likely to last only as long as another event of a more scurrilous sort comes to be. He plants it in one head and it takes wings, Edwin's bastardness forgotten.

Edwin's roots in India are formative. For one, his family stays back. It is not just business interests that tie them to the land, but Lord and Lady Harris's past – and their curious love for the extraordinary circumstances that once found them here. Long after the departure of many, they retain their homes in the mountains – the very ones that become the grounds of his childhood, and later, adulthood adventures. Every morning, when he wakes, breakfast is served to him in his room, which he prefers over the large table where the rest of his garrulous family gathers. He mumbles to himself that it is not the woman who gave birth to him that keeps him returning. Sure, Lady Harris – Mother, he reminds himself – is given to be distant and her eyes seem to almost glide away from him, but didn't she clean his wound when he fell from the apple tree? Didn't she bring him breakfast that first time when Edward's paroxysm for having to share a table with Edwin had eggs and sausages flying from one end of the table to another? This is his family. This is his home.

Edwin is a spirited young boy. The Harris home rests on the face of a mountain, their garden sprawling across many terraced levels. Edwin leaps over balustrades and boundary walls, often spraining a knee or twisting an ankle. Servants, who share the lighter brown of his own skin, run after him – their unhurried but panicked chases always a step too slow. He hunts lean hares darting between trimmed shrubs of plumeria to present to Lady Harris. He wrings their necks himself after he reads of the vegetarian habits of the servants.

At this point, Edwin is rather young, his knowledge of his home limited to the observations of his father's countrymen, who never quite grasp the multitudinous ways of their new world. He often ventures out beyond the mansion grounds to hunt Kalij pheasants – the bird he once overheard his father call 'the most delectable game he ever had'.

Edwin is hopeful, rather desperate, that one day his father and mother will look at him with the same adoration and respect they reserve for Edward. He is not particularly sure of it himself as he would remain for most of his life – until, closer to his deathbed, he will begin the arduous and heartbreaking task of reading through the diaries from the time he started keeping them at the age of ten, and find that he had dedicated his life's work to winning that love that was deliberately withheld from him, and so made aware of his failings to be a fair adult to himself for the past seventy years, shed his first tears for a lost childhood. But for now, he tries harder.

At the Eton of the East, he becomes his masters' favourite. He leads students to do better, to be better. He captains the young lacrosse team and is unbeatable in singles tennis. He even earns a reputation as a formidable bowler, though he loathes the game and the constricting whites it demands. His grades soar. His reading levels unparalleled. When time arrives for his parents to know of his achievements, Dhularam, the estate's manager hears the glowing reviews sitting at the edge of his seat. Edwin feels that the man, scrawny and further appearing thinner for his ill-fitting brown suit, would fly off with pride. 'You will tell Father of my accolades, won't you, Dhularam?' he asks as the man, holding his small hand, snakes his way through a sea of students and parents towards their car.

'Of course, Master Edwin! And I will also tell the kitchen to prepare a cake today. You are one bright star,' Dhularam replies.

From the back seat, Edwin beams at the spark of admiration in Dhularam's eyes.

✿

It is, in fact, Dhularam who plants the first sapling of mountaineering within Edwin. Dhularam, that gaunt man afflicted from an early age with the kinds of ills that take so many at all stages of life. Dhularam, who acquires a taste for

Black Cat cigarettes that Lord Harris has delivered in crates to his cottage, tucked away from their tea estate. Dhularam, who picks Edwin up from day-boarding school each day, and later, from the station when he is exiled to a school in England. Dhularam, who Edwin later realizes was more of a father to him than Harris ever was.

He follows Dhularam into the depths of the tea estate. The manager prefers to inspect each plant himself. The first time Edwin touches the leaves, Dhularam gently tells him to admire from afar. 'The leaves are delicate,' he says. 'They need the touch of a woman.' Throughout the year and the various flushes, Dhularam remains busy, driving his Austin Roadster from one end of the estate to the other. On mornings when Edwin is free from school, he rides his bicycle to Dhularam's cottage. Long before he hears Dhularam's morning songs, he hears the splashing of water. The Roadster collects dust every evening. The terrain is not especially loose, but the car is old and it throws up a cloud of dust that ultimately settles back onto itself.

'Dhularam, hurry!' he shouts. Edwin turns his bicycle into the driveway and, dropping it on the lawn, climbs into the seat of the still-dripping car. That beloved Austin Roadster, which Edwin will inherit after Dhularam's death many years later, is never quite clean enough. There is always mud on the guards, a film of dust on the exhaust and water in the open seats.

Edwin never figures out the routine that keeps Dhularam driving from one part of the estate to another. There is no schedule, no breakdown of what needs to be examined when. Dhularam appears to operate purely by instinct.

'The plants call me,' he once says to Edwin. 'I know which ones need tending.'

These are the same words Edwin will later echo to those who ask after his own mountaineering decisions. 'The mountains beckon me. I know which ones need to be climbed.'

Edwin learns to tell the difference between the tender leaves of the first and second flush. In the busy months of March and April, his weekly excursions to the estate become hectic. The men and women work around the clock, hauling in plucked leaves in baskets and hauling out dried, aromatic ones in sacks.

Through it all, Dhularam never forgets to linger among the women, smoking his cigarettes. In his manner, there is something of a man that Edwin never sees in his father. As if sharing a great secret, he lights cigarettes for the young women, sometimes sharing his own. He whispers into their ears sweet nothings, until the women blush in unison. But Dhularam never forgets Edwin. He brings the boy forward and tells the women of his great achievements.

Edwin does not understand their language. In a rare assertion of rules at home, his father insists that the Indians will always learn their tongue, and that Edwin need not trouble himself with the languages of a country with no global standing. Edwin instead becomes proficient in French and German. Of the workers's many tongues, he knows only a few words – the ones Dhularam often uses when speaking of him – words Edwin supposes are complimentary. *Ziddi. Khushmijaz. Binmaa.*

A visit to the glasshouse one day turns sour. A drunk worker threatens to break the Wardian cases in which experimental tea strains are grown. From the way Dhularam pacifies the man – a gentle hand on the shoulder, promises of a wage discussion, some help delivered to ease the pains of his wife – Edwin understands that such outbursts may be common on the estate. It sprawls across hectares, covers several hills and employs hundreds.

It is also the first time Edwin realizes that Dhularam is a great man, holding the estate together through order and cordial conditions. Later that evening, he doesn't want to part from Dhularam as yet. Nothing waits for him at home – only a little homework and a dinner he can summon at any time. A bell brings food of every kind to his room. Dhularam lets him stay for a cup of tea – Edwin's first. The small cottage is so meticulous and tidy that even Lady Harris, if she ever decided to step into his apartments, would peruse with envy.

Edwin walks around it, cautious, reverent. On a shelf, Dhularam has arranged several volumes; he has had them rebound and colour-coded. Green for murder mysteries. Red for Russian literature. Blue for adventures. Black for philosophy. Edwin runs his finger along the row of blue until it stops at a volume by Frank Smythe.

✿

As is often the case with those of an adventurous spirit, the immediate surroundings – so regular, so mundane – lose all meaning and become inconsequential to Edwin. The expeditious tales of man's resilience feed his hungry mind. A few kilometres from his school, he knows a spot where Kanchenjunga – the great obsession of his hero – reveals itself to mere mortals. Its beatific hand upon the people of the region has not shifted since Edwin was born, but it is only now, through the words of Smythe, that Edwin admires it for its divine glory.

In his father's study, he traces the long range of the Himalayas.

'I will one day climb every Himalayan peak,' he tells his father.

Lord Harris does not look up from his papers. 'You sound like Dhularam with that deplorable accent,' he chides. 'Hima-LAY-uh.'

To Dhularam, he repeats the adventures of Smythe, and later, of Raymond Lambert and George Mallory. As Dhularam bends to inspect a resting fly on a leaf or parks on an empty road to light a cigarette, Edwin lists the peaks of the Himalayas he will one day conquer.

'Hi-Mall-lieyah,' Dhularam corrects.

Edwin's enthusiasm is only briefly shaken by his father's rebuke for what he calls a boorish pronunciation, and one day – for the sake of his father's affection – Edwin decides that his father must know best.

At the Eton of the East, he joins the mountaineering team. The boys are thin-limbed and still in knickers, and their expeditions rarely extend beyond a few kilometres along well-trodden trails. In the sixth form, a guide – a man famed for leading several Swiss alpinist teams into the Himalayas – is invited to speak. Seeing the name of a familiar figure, Edwin sneaks into the auditorium.

In the programme, the man is called, 'A fine specimen of the hard-working Tibetans who age fast for their professions.' *Yes, I see it*, Edwin thinks. *I see what the mountaineers meant*.

His influences, in those days, are men of a certain kind. He absorbs their colonial inclinations without hesitation. To him, every man north of Darjeeling becomes Nepali, and every guide, a Sherpa.

On those short trips to Kamala Falls, climbing the slippery stone steps, Edwin pretends he is conquering the steep slope of the Brenva Face of Mont Blanc. He becomes Frank Smythe, leading a rugged team through an uncharted route. They are the first to ascend by this way, and his name will be written into history. He will stand in his finest Sunday formals and receive a knighthood, and Father and Mother will beam at him with pride, as Dhularam does several times each month.

Edwin is not consulted when his father one day decides it is time for him to study in England. A planned expedition with the school's mountaineering team led by a retired climber to Sandakphu is cancelled. Edwin, reluctant to say a tearful goodbye to Dhularam, refuses to visit him in those final days. The manager rarely brings his car into the Harris's driveway, but Edwin waits at the window nonetheless. Until the moment his trunk is trundled down the stairs and into the hall, then noisily down to the driveway – where, rather than Dhularam, a chauffeur awaits to drive him to the station and then accompany him to Bombay – Edwin keeps his eyes fixed on the road that leads to Dhularam's cottage.

Throughout the journey, he curses himself for not going to see him. At fifteen, he is already aware of the prejudices that keep Dhularam away from the main house. He is allowed only into the smaller office where Lord Harris meets with the four estate managers. Dhularam is never invited into the house, and perhaps wary of the consequences, keeps away himself too.

At the docks, the chauffeur – now in plain pyjamas to bear the heat – follows him as far as allowed. Handing the trunks to a porter, Edwin turns to press a few coins into the man's hand. In return, the chauffeur gives him a large leather bag, and simply says, 'From Dhularam,' before turning around and walking away.

✿

The pursuit of glory is a particularly difficult sickness to grasp. It afflicts the sane and the foolish; able and the incompetent, the loved and the unloved, the lonely and the gregarious. It is here in England that Edwin becomes the man who turns his back on the pleas of the villagers with whom he has lived through tragedy; the man who is unconcerned – even vexed – by the state one of his team has found himself in. At fifteen, the soft roundness that makes children so innocent and gullible begins to leave him, giving way to the tall, loud man whose actions are guided by the dream of being greater than his hero.

In those early years, he still thinks of Dhularam: of his Austin Roadster, the flick of his hand to drop the ash from his cigarettes and the gentle smile that never wavered, no matter how silly Edwin's inquiries became. At sixteen and seventeen, when he returns home for Christmas, it is etiquette that keeps him from running to Dhularam's cottage instead of greeting Mother and Father first. In his dorm, he reads from Dhularam's books of adventure. He keeps them in the same bag that the chauffeur had handed him – seven volumes in total. Every night, he reads a few pages and tells himself, I will write to Dhularam in the morning. But such mornings never arrive.

For a few years, he does not return to India, even if India follows him to Britain. At school, he shares benches with Indians – wealthier, upper-caste boys – who avoid the more aggressive commentaries of their peers. When Edwin tries to speak to them, they call him a *kutcha butcha*. In the presence of the local students, he becomes unseen. Not completely ousted – his father's name protects him – but not included in their mirthful bullying of the brown boys either. A deeper, unfounded hatred seeps into Edwin, until even Dhularam becomes 'coolie'. At the dinner table in the Darjeeling mansion, Lord Harris finally smiles at his bastard son for the first time.

England, the mentions of which he avoids in his younger years, gives wings to his dreams. These are decades of previously uncharted opportunity, when societies reward discovery, and a race for glory sets an unprecedented race and adventures await whosoever wishes to undertake them. On the college bulletin board, Edwin stands beaming at the array of mountaineering clubs to choose from. This is not India, where millions remain occupied with fending for their next meals; where dreams and hopes and spirits are afforded by and awarded to only a few. The mountaineering club raises money for training and expeditions. They welcome the sturdy builds of English blood and turn away the small, frail bodies of Indians. Edwin is quickly accepted for his connections to the subcontinent – home to the tallest mountains in the world. A British team, freshly victorious on Kamet, returns to regale them with stories of their glorious journey. Across the seven seas, the Himalayas feel closer than ever to Edwin.

By the time Edwin turns thirty, he is a revered name in the same clubs he had once joined as a student. For several expeditions, he is rewarded by the government, and the dream of a knighthood begins to appear within reach. A later gripe keeps him from applying again, and he begins leading private expeditions into the Alps. He climbs Mont Blanc and the Matterhorn. He travels to Africa for the first time and conquers Kilimanjaro, where he loses a friend for the first time. The three mountains of Wales become his playgrounds and, to the French who send their own teams onto the highest mountains in the world, Edwin becomes a myth, a legend to be admired, if only in secret.

He traces the trajectory of Smythe's career. The man's life takes on fantastical dimensions in Edwin's mind, until he too discards guides and heavy equipment, even where others advise against it. Each success stokes his ego, until even his most vainglorious tales become mainstays. Edwin pushes further and further. He climbs Kanchenjunga in record time, then again in the middle of a storm – a storm that disappears one friend and shatters the leg of another. Smythe's lean physiognomy, antithetical to the scale of his adventures, Edwin is unable to emulate. He is big-boned and heavily muscled, but he takes on smoking several packs of cigarettes a day. When biographies are written, they will say that Edwin Harris summited dozens of Himalayan peaks with lungs that rattled with a sickly buzz.

It is India that remains in his mind throughout these climbs, regardless of where he finds himself. His mother and Dhularam – who dies before Edwin turns thirty – become unimportant, almost irrelevant in the larger canvas of his life. He never turns his eyes to Everest, the mountain that takes his other hero, Mallory. But most of all, it is the beloved valley of Smythe – the Bhyundar Valley, the Valley of Flowers – that calls Edwin back to the country again and again.

His legacy would be the prolific nature of his expeditions. He would rather burn like a wildfire than flicker like a candle.

Edwin admires her cunning. The first time he sees her peering over the shoulders of others, noting her shifting gaze and the way her eyes widen slightly at the possibility of leaving the village, he is convinced of her conniving nature. It is no surprise then that in the hours before dawn, when the villagers – perhaps eased slightly of their worries after pleading with his team – sleep for the first time in days, the team awakens and slips away towards the military camp. And when they glance over their shoulders, a small shadow follows them into the forest.

In her doggedness, Edwin sees a bit of himself. Her story of a lost sister is, at best, devoid of details she wishes to withhold, and at worst, entirely imaginary in nature. Her destination seems fixed, no other possibilities entertained. And just as the mountains have so often beckoned him – sometimes with modern equipment, sometimes with just his flesh and bones – he only nods for her to keep walking when the others stop to ask.

Still, Edwin is not blind to the fact that a lone woman, not even dressed for the terrain, is an odd sight in these parts of the mountains. Many women – sturdier and handsome – have begun to climb the same mountains men had once conquered alone. Edwin can offer no better explanation than that the men have paved the path for them, their tracks carved into snow, easing the way for the weaker sex. This year, Edwin is the same age Smythe was when he died. This may well be his final expedition in the Valley of Flowers, and he is willing to leave behind anyone who delays or hinders his journey.

Over the years, Edwin has spread his life wider and deeper into these mountains. He has discovered new streams and waterfalls. The injured man – the botanist – who has accompanied him on many of these excursions, has catalogued new plants and flowers, new mosses and ferns that now fatten the volumes of the subcontinent's flora and fauna. Together, they have contributed more to the knowledge of this valley than the man who renamed it for the more sensible tongue of the English. At the age of his hero's death, Edwin too feels no need to continue this life much longer. He plans to walk beyond the valley to a place marked on his map, previously unexplored and waiting for his arrival. He is finishing his hero's work, and if this is his final foray, then disaster and injury will not be what holds him back.

When he learns that the botanist has twisted his ankle, Edwin briefly considers leaving him behind. The village and the climbers have developed the same problem – hungry, without belongings, stripped of direction. Perhaps the botanist could find some comfort among those who now suffer alike. But each time they have climbed the valley together, the botanist has made discoveries that keep the Royal Society at their doors. Edwin could abandon him, but the others are mere climbers, chasing mountains for thrill and adrenaline. There is no greater purpose to their climbs than boasting to a girl in a pub, or to mothers who never loved them for failing their school exams. The botanist, however, shares that singular passion – the one that keeps men in mad pursuit, even when the world conspires against them.

Edwin believes the botanist will understand. Yes, they will be slower, and the man may worsen his injury in the process, but when Edwin whispers to him what awaits at the end, the botanist rises and begins to walk small circuits around the mound. If on the way, either the botanist or the woman prompt trouble, he would not hesitate to push them off the edge of a cliff, or abandon them as he has now abandoned the village.

NINETEEN

She has spent only a few hours with Edwin before she realizes that the man is inclined towards mad decisions. The village – or rather the ruined remains of it – recedes behind them as they journey towards the military camp. Often, she looks over her shoulder. The mound is now shielded by a grove of pine, but the expanse of the village clears as they climb. In those hours of breaking dawn, no structure is discernible. A blurring crescent moon is sometimes visible on the river that runs through the streets and alleys of the village. It appears and disappears behind dark clouds, and she suspects that the rain that has been so kind in the days after the flood will now return with a vengeance for having to subside for so long.

The injured, limping man walks the slowest. One of the guides keeps a gentle arm around his straining body, but the guide himself is thin and short, and the larger figure of the climber leans uneasily against him. Towards the front, Edwin grumbles every few seconds. In his frustration, he – the climber, the admirer of the Himalayas – fails to witness the undulating landscape that passes by unnoticed before his eyes. Sometimes she catches up with him, but the words he mutters under his breath are not for her ears, meant rather to quell the bitterness he feels towards his companion.

She suspects that the injured man will soon be left behind – like the village, like she has so often been in the vast passage of a short life. Those who thunder towards destinations simply forget the ones who slow them on their journeys. Their worries and hurts, their dissatisfactions are of no consequence to others. They become observers barricaded behind boxes of glass, their pleas and requests, like those of the villagers, ignored. Life and its various roadblocks and crossings are denied to them. The joys and intimacy of a well-lived existence are denied to them. They remain standing while the world passes around them, until, from where they stay standing, it passes them one final time.

In the fate that is to be of the injured man, that spark of rare kinship begins to kindle. There are no words she can offer, nor would her help ease the pain of his failing body. When he purses his lips to swallow a whimper, she too mirrors the painful pressing of his mouth into his teeth. Perhaps he is aware of the turmoil that now plagues his friend. They have climbed several mountains together, across both hemispheres, from one continent to another. It is vanity, a need to stand the test of time, to become a name that remains in the memories of many generations that drives Edwin on these expeditions to the Himalayas. He has been his trusted friend, the brains to his brute. He adds Edwin's name to papers describing his discoveries. He thanks and appreciates the man in his published articles.

On Kilimanjaro, where Edwin and he climb together for the first time, a man falls off a short cliff. It is still close to the base camp, and if allowed a day's journey back, the man could be provided assistance. Edwin tells the men to keep moving ahead, to scout the next climb while he tends to the fallen. The man's tibia breaks in the middle, spearing through flesh and skin to lie exposed to the cold air. 'We will decide then who returns with our friend,' Edwin says. A few hours later, having lost very little time, the team finds Edwin sitting alone. 'I must have rested my eyes for only a few minutes, but when I awoke, he was nowhere to be seen,' he mumbles. It is concluded that the man was perhaps buried in snow, as so often happens to those who pass on glaciers. Sometimes they crawl towards their nearest camp and are lost on the way. Edwin is never suspected by the others, but his insistence on continuing the climb leaves the now-injured man forever uncertain of his friend.

She hopes that the injured man will be left behind at the military camp. A few feet ahead, in a large clearing, they spot the wire mesh of its entrance. Edwin is familiar with the soldiers near the gates. At a command, the others remain behind, only faintly hearing the words Edwin shares with them. When he tells them of the village, several other soldiers join. They bring the other climbers and her into the conversation, asking about the event as if it is so far in the past that only the faintest memories of it could be recalled with much strain.

Do you remember how many people died? Lost? Hurt? Any homes that might have survived?

Edwin's abrupt benevolence lasts only so long. When the soldiers dissipate to bring out horses and vehicles, when duty-bound in the face of disaster they move swiftly to serve those they had previously ignored, Edwin's palpable anger at the same soldiers, who now neglect his requests of some food for their journey and knowledge to guide them onto the other route to the valley, buzzes in the air around the climbers. They shift uneasily on their feet, avoiding the eyes of others. It is in this moment that she learns of Edwin's madness.

Edwin paces the ground running along the entrance of the camp like a caged animal. His steps thud harder onto the brown earth with every round. A vehicle honks at him when he refuses to move. A soldier leans out and curses the entire group. When the people ask if they may wait inside, Edwin responds with a firm no.

'We must be on our way as soon as possible,' he explains.

The injured man is asked no questions, and when enquired after, Edwin refuses to provide any explanation.

The most horrendous events of a man's existence are often rendered by a lack of choice; the most atrocious mutilations carried out through the choices made by others. Like the uncle's choice to unleash his violence on a child. Like Damodar Pradhan's decision to turn a deaf ear to his wife's needs. Like her choice to bury Leela's child. The choice is thus made for the injured man.

When the camp seems to have emptied of most of its people, a few from the kitchen arrive with food and water. To Edwin, they explain the terrain. They will need to turn north-east into the jungle for a couple of days, beyond which the river cutting into the valley will become visible.

'Follow it upstream,' the cook says.

When he mentions a village beyond the valley of flowers, Edwin and the climbers look to her. They believe her lie.

'What of your friend?' the cook asks. He points towards the sleeping figure.

'He is of the sturdy breed,' Edwin replies.

✿

They reach the promised jungle before dusk. Under the thick canopy, the light fails to enter, reaching only in streaks from the sleeping sun that filters between the crowns. The injured climber and his helper arrive some hours later. Around a small bonfire, Edwin distributes packets of roti, soggy and oily from the sabzi they cradle. There are tins and cans of beans and sardines among the salvaged equipment.

'We will ask for food from the villages until there are no more villages on the way,' Edwin responds to a younger climber's query.

Of his friend, limping and feverish, Edwin forgets. When they appear from the thick of the forest, the sharpness of their figures blurred in the shadows of the night, he only passes them the wrapped food and says, 'If you had arrived earlier, you could have seen some strange gymnosperms.'

He never looks up from his meal, and the other climbers follow suit, avoiding the accusing eyes of the sherpa, who pants his way into the camp. She is surprised by the gentleness with which the man lowers the climber onto a log. It is the kind of unexpected care she too once learnt to receive, though she doubts the injured man has the awareness or alertness left to protest. He remains limp, swaying slightly where he sits.

Until she retires into Edwin's tent, where the two lie cramped together, their backs to one another – she in a mackintosh coat

Edwin gives her, and he in a green sleeping bag – she believes that the injured man remains outside, with the wrapped food still in hand that he had made no move to eat.

That first night in the forest, she is lulled to sleep by the soft patter of rain on the plastic covering of the tent. Erratic gusts of wind, crushed to gentle breezes by the tall trees, creep in beneath the edges of the shelter and settle into her bones. At the edge of the river, the beast too shivers with the wind. The journey to the river has been arduous, the path of pebbles digging cruelly into its wound. From the tattered flesh, there rises such a stench that if it wasn't for the festering gash it has been observing and licking, the beast might have suspected danger lurking close.

At the raised banks, it lolls its tongue in breathlessness. Its insides feel feverish, as if sweat breaks out in the space between its heart and stomach, between its tendons, as if instead of life force, beading perspiration rubs between bones. Sharp stones and coarse soil dig into its flesh but the river is only a few feet away. In a sprint, it drops from the bank and towards the water. It howls in agony – the pain rising from the paw into its spine – but then the water suddenly sneaks between its claws, and sprays against its chin and neck. The beast collapses into the river. Its current is just beginning to swell.

In the tent, she wakes with a jolt. Her heart beats a loud rhythm between her ears. Outside, the rain has picked up but the warmth of Edwin's body still lingers in the small enclosure. When she rolls onto her back to spy at his sleeping figure, her stomach coils uncomfortably. It has been many days since she last ate properly, and the food from the military camp sits uneasily in her. She twists and shifts – both to cease the sensation in her roiling belly and to find Edwin – but the sleeping bag is turning cold.

Amid the noise of rain falling over several plastic tents and the low grumble of rain clouds, she hears words. Around the bonfire, now doused, the climbers and sherpas gather around in a tight circle. Edwin sits on the ground across from the injured man. He has not moved since they retired into the tents, his hair pasted to his forehead, rain dripping from it like a leaky faucet. Edwin places a hand on the man's shoulder and shakes him gently. The helper, standing behind him, swats Edwin's hand away with surprising force.

She does not need to understand the words to sense that an argument brews between them both. She catches some phrases, some words, inflections and accents of anger and disappointment – tinged with a need for action. Perhaps the sherpas want to return to the military camp where the injured man could still be treated. But Edwin only places his hand again on his friend's shoulder – allowing a man who can barely lift himself to decide both his fate and the future of Edwin's expedition.

✿

The group awakes to Edwin's frantic activity outside the tents. Near the damp bonfire, he empties the contents of his bags. Crouched on a rock, he repacks them, mindful not to let steel strike against steel, until the early morning sounds of a forest freed from rain are drowned by the clatter.

Through the night, the cramps in her stomach worsen until she too whimpers like the beast. The beast itself does not appear in her dreams again, and she believes it has not risen from its slumber in the shallow river. It is only with one hand placed before the other that she crawls out of the tent. At her appearance, Edwin grumbles meanly under his breath. Perhaps she has slept longer than necessary, but in the clearing, only four people have gathered.

It is still the morning hours. Dew and raindrops rest on grass and cycads. From the canopy above, barbets and thrushes call out meekly. They are suspicious of the receded rains, their conversations cautious, gauging its return. When she glances over her shoulder, she catches a flash of white plumage, but before she can turn to look again, the white bird from the hunter's memoir has flown into the deep of the forest.

Edwin is in a hurry to be on his way. Their journey is far from over. This part of the valley is only one leg. Beyond the valley of flowers, where carpets of orange and purple stretch towards the horizon, till the mountains appear to sway with mirth beneath the gentle breeze of the Himalayas, there is still a rather long way to the undiscovered land Edwin has set his mind on.

Of his injured friend, he makes no mention. It is simply understood that the man will soon awake from his fevered, dying sleep and follow, taking the rear until he can no longer go on.

When Edwin hands her another packed roti, she can only retch. The unfamiliar sensation of something crawling within her leaves little room for appetite, though she finds that in that moment, she desires nothing more than a few morsels to return strength to her body and will to her mind. In these years of a largely unfulfilled life, her struggles and hurts have remained of a more ephemeral nature. She wakes with an aching body that is still in its prime and does so only for the turmoil that berates her even in her sleep. Her mind chatters with the loudness of an incensed and protesting crowd. Her loneliness cocoons her in a poisonous embrace. It is that small stroke of luck, she believes, that keeps her afloat, her poverty confined to the mind, her hunger only of a cerebral kind.

Now her stomach roils with a different kind of poison – the kind that threatens to deplete the last of her being. To the climbers, she wishes to express the doubts. Perhaps they too stand at the precipice of this illness but she is afraid of being left behind, just as Edwin, she suspects, is about to leave his injured friend.

Their time in the forest is short. When the canopy breaks to reveal a cloudy sky and tops of hills stretching from one to another, Edwin first whines, frustrated at the day they have lost, then breaks into a run across the open ground. He skips over strewn rocks, his hands stretched at his sides. His laughter is carried with the wind, and even the climbers, previously concerned for the one they carry, now smile at the unbridled joy that runs through their leader.

One, then two, then the whole group, save for her and the two others, run down through the forest and into the clearing. Carpets of lush green dotted with plumeria and poppy stretch as far as the eyes can see. A beaten path cuts through the hills, its curves rising and hiding with the contours of the mountains. At the edge of the forest, the injured man pants, his eyes rooted to the infinite steps before him.

Much to Edwin's chagrin, rains begin while they are still crossing the open expanse of the hilltops. Though it is only midday, dark clouds dim the light and a light drizzle dampens the previous excitement that had briefly gripped the climbers.

'We must reach the river today,' Edwin commands.

They still have several kilometres to descend before they climb another mountain that would finally lead them into the valley of Edwin's obsession and the final resting place of she and the beast.

The group is forced to hurry when the laden clouds finally unleash in a torrent. The soft drizzle turns to a downpour. Rain thunders down in a storm. Lightning splits the sky in streaks of purple. The wind takes up soon enough, and the clearing, so loved and enjoyed, turns into a threat. Edwin leads the group down the hill face. In some distance, hidden behind undergrowth and sparse woods, the river becomes visible through shifting gaps.

He reaches the bank first, letting his feet slip over the pebbled slope. The river here is shallow, swimming lazily after its battering path from the high mountains and the harder still path it will take into the lower Himalayas. At its banks, Edwin begins the practised task of pitching tents.

From within the woods that the remaining group has yet to cover, she cannot help but admire the promptness of his movements. He has perfected the art, the nuances of his passions, and each grip of his fingers, each step of his feet adds to the urgency of the moment. In this admiration, she begins to understand Edwin's vexation. In another time, she might have been familiar with this man – not through affection, but through his achievements. His contributions are not to humanity, but to the wild arts of the world that rely on the thrill of glory rather than some vestigial contribution to mankind. She is not aware of the injured man's contribution to botany, and if she had known, she would have not absorbed Edwin's frustration as she does in the moment.

In this brief excitement, she forgets the clawing ache in her stomach that skips and skirts around the illness now blooming inside her. On the final stretch to the river, she runs like the beast in her dream. Reaching the same edge it had touched the night before, she jumps off, then drops into the water. Against the thundering rain and accompanying winds, the chill that now rests in the folds of her clothes and on the surface of her body, the river is warm and comforting. There is not enough depth to float and she is wary of treading further than the shallow spots lest she be swept away in a moment of inattention. A rock digs into her neck. It is sharp and smooth, and instead of sitting up, she feels for it gingerly with her hands. Towards the weeping skies, she lifts her hand. In it, she holds the pearlescent claw of a leopard.

That night, she discards her clothes. There is no moment of relief from the rain to dry or a bonfire to warm them. In Edwin's coat, she buries herself into the side of the tent, pressing its ends with half her body. It is not warm, nor do the thunderclaps that shake them from sleep promise hope for the morning. Edwin barely sleeps either. He twists and turns in his sleeping bag, bothered by the noise that begins as one of a downpour and becomes the eerie slapping horror of a storm. Near the flaps of the tent, he moves the zip up and down until it snags in the fabric. He slaps at it in rising anguish.

She is unable to discern this odd display of his inner workings. Most people are rather ashamed to lay bare the baser emotions that comprise chunks of their existence. Kumar, who was angered by the love that his father had withheld from him, hid it under the veil of distance. Aarav, saddened by the early demise of a worshipped hero, masked it with achievement. Leela, deprived of a childhood, discarded it further in her benevolence. Edwin's gradually increasing desperation to conquer this valley is raw and painful to watch.

She herself hides behind imaginations and concoctions – acceptable tales easy to swallow for apprehensive strangers.

Over Edwin's shoulder, she peers out at the sheet of rain. It leaves the dark forest in abysmal shadows. Right outside, not even the grass or pebbled terrain they pitch their tent on escapes these shadows. Edwin's frantic activity in the cramped space keeps her from falling asleep. This close to the beast and cradling the claw to her breast, she believes that when the rain relents, she will find the one she has chased for so long. It has been a voyage of many days, spread over many lifetimes; of a stroke of a brush here and a scribbling of fate there. Through cities of unreasonable paces, to shelters of tranquility; betrayal, death, and lost and denied companionships, it is the beast that has kept her on the path.

Before she reaches the valley towards which the climbers fix their eyes and the beast presumably made its way, she wants to see its dirty coat and mangled paw through its own eyes once again.

It is waiting.

This long trek into an unknown, unreasonable forest has been as much to draw as to escape that which follows it. It is no more than a lingering sensation, like the hair on the back of neck standing when shadows tremble where they shouldn't, or when a young woman hurries through the streets at night and faintly hears steps that do not belong behind her. It is that which keeps children up at night and the older from closing their eyes for too long.

In the darkness, it licks a dirty paw. It is by instinct, even though there is no reason to do so. The flesh is infested with maggots and the spikes on its tongue displace them from their burrows and into other spots. Behind its eyes, it feels a fever – the kind of heat that might burn away even the skin on an animal. It reaches the valley in the darkest of hours. Its nose picks no scents. Its ears hear no tell-tale signs of opening skies.

One moment it is dragging itself over grass and soil, and another, its tired paws hit slippery stone. It does not remember crawling to this cover of granite. In her sleep, it is quiet. The beast begins its final rest, waking only once to smell the ancient dirt that lies buried deep in the eroded texture of the granite.

Unbeknownst to her, the injured climber – who has lain in fevered sleep, whispering and muttering for hours – finally falls silent.

TWENTY

The first time she sees death is not on a person. It is one of the dozens of cats that often jump into their backyard over towering walls. There are at least thirteen that she recognizes by names – simple to remember, colour-coded: Bhuri, Kalu, Safeda – and the rest that she is still learning to tell apart. The backyard is always alive with the howling noises of mating cats and fighting cats and playing cats. On this day, it remains quiet. Under an untrimmed champa, a cat the size of her arm sits with her eyes closed. Around her, several kittens circle, unsure. When she gets closer, she doesn't recognize Bhuri. Her face of feline mischief is stripped of all the suppleness that makes flesh alive. Her face is drawn, her eyes receded deep into her skull. From her nose and mouth, snot and phlegm and blood – all mingled in one discoloured discharge – drips into the scraggly hair on her chin. In a nostril, a feather from a pigeon sticks out. Between her sharp canines, threads of red fabric. Bhuri is not yet dead, but she, at six, knows this is the end. When Bhuri hears the girl's running feet, she can only raise her head so much before releasing a cry – of help or in pain, or a plea for relief. She brings Bhuri into her room. In the night, her cries grow louder, though once, she gets to her feet as if released from the grip of death. She walks to a pail of water and drinks from it for many seconds. When she stretches, first her hind legs, then the front, she thinks Bhuri might live. In the morning, under the window where she professes her greatest desires to her diary, a trail of urine shines under the sunlight. Bhuri lies on her side, her black and brown coat like a blanket of topaz. From her bed, she can see the convex bulge of her open eyes. The illness has left, Bhuri's once beautiful face at least mercifully returned to its painless state. It is, however, the lack of movement – no twitching whiskers or blinking eyes or flicking ears – that takes her by surprise. There is no Bhuri in that absolute stillness.

At the banks, where the river is now flowing closer to her tent, when she finds the injured man, it is that absolute stillness that she notices – right after she realizes that she has indeed been abandoned. The climbers and tents are gone. Inside, she is overwhelmed with a wave of gratitude for being left this cover, but the rain has stopped. Outside, she observes the rising levels of the river, looking for the least treacherous way to the other side. She notices a different kind of stillness first. At a distance, she squats into the river to relieve herself, and when she rises, it is the absence of that coiling pain in the pit of her stomach that takes her by surprise. She is Bhuri, stretching her legs for her last drink of water.

On her short walk back to the tent, she rankles at her predicament. Edwin leaves behind the tent, but forgets food. Perhaps it is her reluctance to eat that makes him do so, but the back of her eyes sting anyway. It isn't until she sees a huddled figure where one tent had been that her bitterness leaves her. She hurries to it, drawn to its calm and fixedness. It does not occur to her that it could be the injured man, left behind like she is. He is cold but still soft to the touch, his eyes ugly and protruding. She tries to yank his eyelids down, but they part slowly again. She looks over her shoulders. *Maybe the others are not so far*, she thinks. When she rises, she believes she is only following the climbers onto their trail. She will hail them back to help their friend. It is as if thinking the words would offend the dead man and make him weep from loneliness.

✿

Her mother visits her at her college only once. A dengue outbreak takes hundreds of students, and though reluctant, she writes a letter when the nurses insist. By her bedside, her mother asks her to let go of her anger. It is unprompted, even unnecessary, when she, writhing in fever, can barely string thoughts together. 'Those who come to live,' her mother says, 'are cursed with sorrow and loneliness. If one holds on to this anger, the loneliness drowns them so much faster.' Her own sorrow and loneliness the mother tucks between the folds of her stomach and the creases of her face, in the callouses on her hand.

The mother is rather small and docile, masterful and practised in averting her gaze. She remains so for most of her life. She upholds childlike beliefs – that if a butterfly flies from its cocoon and dies, then it is to itself that it brings that fate. Her life of subservience and sacrifice are her badges of honour – the only ones she can pass on to her daughters. It is the daughters, then, who entice their ill luck. On the hospital bed, she learns there is nothing her mother could give her, and perhaps there is nothing she could provide her mother either. She is burdened by a hostile weight, and when she refuses to carry that of her mother, it leaves a chasm between them.

She is in no hurry to meet the beast. It is there, just a few steps ahead. It leaves the cave in one last burst of energy, perhaps mustered from the small rainbows that rise from the earth and the scent of billions of blooming flowers floating upwards from the valley before it. She smells its rotting presence over those from the valley. It is strong, feral in the granite cover. Much like Bhuri – and now, the beast – her hunger and exhaustion give way to the last vestiges of strength.

The bushes are tall, rising up to her chin. Through the dense foliage, she hears a small roar. It is clear and discernible, as if she is dreaming through its eyes again. As if they have both found themselves in the place they had decided to meet. From the edge of the granite cover, she looks over at the valley glimmering under the sun. On the farthest mountain, a small line moves. Edwin has crossed the valley.

She crosses the narrow path from the cave and parts the tender plants of balsam. The path slopes down, the balsam mixing with poppies and orchids of orange and pink. The brilliant carpet of velvet flowers is blinding, overwhelming to the child within her who had dreamt of these places. The child would have laughed and twirled, plucked a few and stitched them into the hem of her frock. She would have jumped and dropped to the ground, pretended to swim in this sea of colours. She could do it too – but right there in the middle lies the leopard.

Her face, marked with spots of copper and black, is that of Bhuri – drawn into a mask of pain and death. Her eyes are sunk deep into their sockets. Her skin is grey and sickly under her matted coat, bloodied with maggots that have dug their premature way into her flesh. She lies on her side, her paws outstretched in her direction. An injured paw rests protectively over a black and dirty stump.

The leopard gazes at her lazily. The groans that had beckoned her from the granite cover become whimpers. The leopard knows it is the shadows that have come to meet her, and the whimpers are of mercy. When she stops approaching, the leopard groans – loud and deep, surprising in its intensity. She jumps back, careful of the beast before her, only to realize that she is as helpless as the child she had been under her uncle's gaze. Lost are her powerful claws that could rip through men and the jaws that could bite through jugulars. She is no more a beast than the child that was taken from its cradle. She is no more the mythical creature of legends. She is a pathetic animal, an unsuspecting actor in the story of another. In a curious moment of cruelty, she removes the claw from the pocket of Edwin's coat and rolls it towards the leopard. She watches the claw tumble on the ground, her eyes following its trajectory. She stares at it with longing before reverting her gaze to the woman.

She lowers herself to the ground, slowly and painfully, her heart tugging at her moment of weakness. The leopard is only a hand's width from her, and lying side by side, the two stretch almost to the same length. In some strange time, she must have been a majestic creature, a terror of such strength and beauty that others must have frozen under her power. Her eyes still shine with that glory and pride.

She never breaks her gaze.

ACKNOWLEDGEMENTS

It takes a village to raise a child and it took a village to write this book. First and foremost, my greatest gratitude to my friend Rupal Vyas, without whose motivation this book would have never reached Pan Macmillan India's inbox, let alone into your hands. To my unwavering support system – Arunima Kapoor, Priyanka Prasad, Shivranjani Singh, Ira Kapoor, Suvarna Tiwari, Gurneet Aujla, Namita Vora. Women of such kindness and calibre that each day with them is a gift.

To the Pan Macmillan India's team. Shreyoshee Bandyopadhyay and Teesta Guha Sarkar for championing this book with a greater conviction and belief than I could ever imagine. To Pujitha Krishnan for seeing it to such an incredible conclusion. To Pooja, Udyotna, Divyanshi and Saburi for every second that you have put into polishing this book and celebrating it out in the world. No amount of thanks is enough.

To the Family Fables team which was less of a workplace and more a place of learning and growing with the greatest kind of people.

To my parents, for introducing me to my first book. It has been a rough ride and there is a long way to go, but I can only imagine what a task it must have been to raise such a loud-mouthed, rebellious child. Thank you.

Lastly, to all the readers. Thank you for coming with me on this journey. I hope to see you soon again on another.